"I'm Asking You to Go Steady,"

Mark says.

Your eyes are filled with tears. You want to run around the table and hug him. It would be wonderful to go steady with Mark. He is the most considerate person you have ever met in your life.

But all summer, while you were losing weight, while Mark was dreaming about you, you were thinking about how exciting it would be to be thin and attractive . . . and popular. Mark is really the only guy you have ever dated. You owe it to yourself to go out with other guys.

Your head is bouncing back and forth. *Mark is an extraordinary human being,* you think. *And he likes me for who I am, not what I look like.*

Will you decide to go steady with Mark? Or will you choose to remain free to date other boys?

FOLLOW YOUR HEART ROMANCES for you to enjoy

#1 SUMMER IN THE SUN
#2 BOYS! BOYS! BOYS!

Available from ARCHWAY paperbacks

Follow Your Heart Romance   # 2

Boys!
Boys! Boys!

Jan Gelman

AN ARCHWAY PAPERBACK
PUBLISHED BY POCKET BOOKS NEW•YORK

This novel is a work of fiction. Names, characters, places and incidents are either the product of the author's imagination or are used fictitiously. Any resemblance to actual events or locales or persons, living or dead, is entirely coincidental.

AN ARCHWAY PAPERBACK *Original*

An Archway Paperback published by
POCKET BOOKS, a Simon & Schuster division of
GULF & WESTERN CORPORATION
1230 Avenue of the Americas, New York, N.Y. 10020

ISBN: 0-671-46730-1

First Archway Paperback printing May, 1983

10 9 8 7 6 5 4 3 2 1

AN ARCHWAY PAPERBACK and colophon are trademarks of Simon & Schuster.

FOLLOW YOUR HEART is a trademark of Simon & Schuster.

Printed in the U.S.A.

IL 5+

*For
Cathy, Nancy,
Caroline, Sarah,
and Arpiné*

Read This First!

Boys! Boys! Boys! is not an ordinary romance book. It will not make sense if you try to read the pages consecutively. Instead, read until you come to a choice. Then follow your choice to the page indicated. Again, read until you come to a choice; then follow the instructions.

When you reach an ending, the book is not over. Just go back to the beginning and make different choices. You can lose—but only temporarily. If you've really messed up, don't worry. There is always another chance.

So follow your heart, read your way to romance, and have a good time.

You have just returned from a summer in New Hampshire where you lived on blueberries and wild greens and an occasional brook trout. When you left home, you were 25 pounds overweight—somewhere between plump and fat. Now you have a fabulous figure.

Ever since you can remember, you have dreamed of being thin. You have spent hours in your room turning the pages of *Seventeen* magazine, looking at the models and wondering what it must feel like to be so slim. You have stood in front of the mirror sucking in your cheeks, cinching your waist, cutting off your fat thighs with your hands in an effort to see yourself thin. You have always known that if only you were thin, the world would be perfect.

Finally you've done it. Suddenly eyes that never focused on you before, follow you down the street. You put on a bikini the other day and when you squinted, you could actually see a model in the mirror.

(continued on page 2)

Then why are you so frightened to go back to school? The thought of facing all those people who knew you as a fat person absolutely terrifies you. You wonder how they will react, what they will say, what you will say.

You may have lost a lot of weight on the outside, but inside you are still the same insecure, over-weight girl who left.

When you arrive home you are presented with two messages. The first is that Coach Thomas, the football coach at your high school, is having a team meeting Friday afternoon. You and your friend Jill have agreed to be team managers and you are in-vited to attend. The thought of strutting your new body before the football team terrifies and excites you.

The second message is from someone named Mrs. Conroy. You have never heard of her. She is a personal friend of your photography teacher and wants to hire you to take pictures at the Conroy family reunion Friday afternoon. She will pay you $50.00, and maybe more if she orders extra prints. You desperately need the money since none of your old clothes fit your new body.

If you go to the meeting, turn to page 3.

If you take the job, turn to page 7.

Jill convinces you to go to the meeting.

"What do you mean *should* you go or not? Did you agree to be manager?"

"Okay, okay. I hear you," you say. "Pick me up at three."

At two o'clock on Friday you start to get ready. You shower and blow-dry your hair. Then you stand in front of your closet trying to decide what to wear.

You choose a pair of lavender-and-white striped shorts and a white shirt. Last summer, you never even put on a pair of shorts. You couldn't stand the thought of showing your fat thighs. Now you're standing in front of the mirror admiring your new look. You wonder how the football team is going to react. Will they notice? And if they make comments, what are you supposed to say? It's all so new and scary.

When you think about the football team, the only one you can picture is John, the quarterback. He was always nice to you last year when you and Jill kept score and took statistics at the football games. He used to call you the Bobbsey Twins, even though you don't look at all alike.

Like almost every other girl in the school, you had a crush on him. You knew, of course, that you didn't have a chance; you were so out of it.

Just thinking about John makes your heart pound—his big deep-brown eyes. Over the summer, John's cheerleader girlfriend moved to New

(continued on page 4)

York. Now he's fair game for you and the six million other girls who are in love with him.

Your daydream is interrupted by the phone. "Pick you up in fifteen minutes," says Jill.

You take one glance in the mirror. Is that image looking back really you? You still can't believe it. You rush downstairs for a quick lunch but you decide to skip it altogether. You want to look as thin as possible. You are just finishing a note to your parents telling them where you are when the horn honks.

"Look at you," says Jill as you climb into her yellow Mustang. "I've never seen you in shorts before. You look fabulous. I can't believe it."

"Thanks, you look terrific too," you say. Jill is probably the most beautiful person you've ever seen. Her long dark-brown hair frames her high cheekbones and green eyes. She is about 5'6" tall and has a thin muscular build. A lot of people think she's stuck-up, but you know that she just has a mind of her own. She's a terrific friend.

The most important thing to Jill is getting into Harvard. She makes straight As, is active in about five different school organizations, and spends most of her free time reading. It always amazes you how the two of you have been best friends for five years. You are completely different. Right now you aren't even sure you want to go to college at all. You want to become a photographer, and college seems completely irrelevant.

(continued on page 5)

"Hey," Jill says. "Have you talked to Mark since you've been back? He never stopped telling me how much he missed you."

"He called, but I wasn't home. I'll call him tonight," you say.

You and Mark have known each other for three years—ever since you met in the photography class at the Y. Mark is incredibly talented. He's won all sorts of prizes for his black-and-white nature studies. And you and he have spent hours talking photography, developing and printing together, and sometimes holding hands in a warm, easy way. He's the only guy you've ever felt comfortable with, and he's always been there to help you through your tough times and to laugh with you through your good times.

When you think about Mark, you feel warm and good all over. His voice is soft and velvety and he has an artistic, romantic soul. Once he arrived at your front door with a handful of violets. "Happy Tuesday," he said, smiling. Another time, when he knew you were depressed, he dressed his little brother in a Superman costume and sent him over with a gift-wrapped chocolate bar.

You are never quite sure what to expect from Mark, and you love his unpredictability. He's a very special person and you know that he'll be your friend forever. He makes you feel happy that you're you.

When you think about John, something al-

(continued on page 6)

together different happens to you. Instead of being comfortable, you feel excited. Instead of calm, there is a storm inside you.

"One, two, three, four. Two, two, three, four . . ."

Your thoughts are interrupted as Jill pulls into the parking lot. The football team is finishing its exercises and marching toward the locker room.

"Six, two, three, four. Seven, two, three, four . . ."

Suddenly you feel a knot in your stomach and beads of sweat on your forehead. The idea of facing all those guys terrifies you. You might look different but you're the same inside, and you still don't know how to act around boys—except Mark, of course.

"I can't do it. I'm not going!" you say.

"Oh, come on. You look great. You're gonna have them falling at your feet," Jill says.

"I can't. Coach Thomas doesn't know we're coming. Let's just see a movie or something. Please, Jill."

"You're being idiotic," Jill says. "But I'll support you if you're really scared. Just remember, Coach Thomas is counting on us."

___

If you go to the meeting, turn to page 15.

If you leave, turn to page 10.

You decide that you don't want to deal with the football team and old friends right now; and besides, you really need the money. You call Mrs. Conroy and tell her that you will take pictures at her reunion.

Friday afternoon you collect your equipment and drive to the Conroys. You are about to make a left into the driveway when an orange Porsche swings in from the other direction. You nearly crash.

"After you, my dear," calls an incredibly handsome guy just a little older than you. He backs his convertible out and pulls in behind you.

As you are emptying the cameras and flashes and other equipment from your trunk, he walks over.

His black hair is layer-cut and styled, and probably blown dry. The soft look of his hair is a beautiful complement to his high cheekbones and wide square jaw.

"Can I give you a hand?" he asks. *He has to be a movie star,* you think. His navy blue blazer and white pants give him that clean-cut, sharp look that you love.

"Thanks," you say and hand him your tripod and film case. When his hand accidentally touches yours, you feel goosebumps up your arm. He smiles and walks toward the front door. His eyes are almost as dark as his hair, and there's a mysterious sparkle in them.

You are greeted at the door by a middle-aged woman. "Come in," she says. She takes your hand

(continued on page 8)

and leads you into a large living room tastefully decorated with antiques.

"You can leave all of your stuff in here. I'll show you around the house; then we'll get you set up outside. The guests won't be arriving for about an hour, so there's plenty of time."

When you look around, you see your tripod and film case on the couch, but there's no sign of your mysterious dream man.

"Oh, by the way," says Mrs. Conroy, "my husband and I own a wholesale clothing business. If you would rather come shopping instead of getting the $50, you are welcome to. The retail value of the clothes would come to more than $100 when you're finished."

"Great," you say. "I'm desperate for a new wardrobe."

"We'll try to do it someday next week," says Mrs. Conroy as you follow her outside into a huge backyard.

Along the back wall of the house there is a buffet table filled with roast beef, corned beef, and turkey. There are large bowls of potato salad, coleslaw, carrot salad, and other vegetables.

In the middle of the table sits a long centerpiece made of carved vegetables. There are radishes cut into roses, turnips shaped like lilies, cucumbers that resemble tropical flowers. You have never seen anything so unique. *Great picture,* you think and you decide that the best angle would be from up

(continued on page 9)

high. Mrs. Conroy gets you a ladder and you climb up.

As you are snapping the picture, you see a dog running straight for the cold cuts.

"Hey," you scream. But you are too late. In seconds, the whole tray of roast beef, corned beef and turkey is on the grass. The Labrador retriever is gobbling up the Conroy family dinner.

"Oh my goodness . . . I don't believe it," screams Mrs. Conroy. "What am I going to do?!"

Since there is nothing much that anyone can do, you take pictures of the chaos.

"Get over here, Roger!" a male voice roars. Your dark-haired Romeo walks over and grabs the dog. "Look what you did!" he says, hitting the dog on the nose. You click away.

"Ricky, what am I going to do?" Mrs. Conroy moans. She is frantically picking up the ruined meat from the ground. "We've got to get some more food and I've got too much to do. Everyone will be here soon."

You really don't have anything to do until the people arrive.

If you offer to get some more cold cuts, turn to page 22.

If you decide to stick to your job, turn to page 13.

"I can't do it," you say.

"Okay," Jill says. "Let's go get a soda." You drive to the diner up the street and sit down in a booth.

"Thanks, Jill," you say. "I don't know what I'd do without you."

"Hey, don't worry about it," she says. "You've gone through a lot of changes and you need some time to work things out."

You and Jill sit in the diner for more than an hour, sipping your diet sodas and catching up on the details of your summers. Jill seems just a little uneasy, as if she wants to tell you something but can't quite get it out. You have no idea what could be upsetting her, and you know it would be futile to try to squeeze it out. *Oh, well,* you think, *when she's ready, she'll tell me.*

"Oh, I almost forgot," says Jill as you are getting ready to leave. "I want to drive to Harvard a week from Wednesday just to look at the campus and the Cambridge scene. Will you go with me?"

"Sure," you say. You've never been to Cambridge.

"Great," says Jill. "That'll give us six hours of talking, three up and three back. We can do a lot of catching up."

"I have to go to the ladies' room before we go," you say as Jill pays the cashier.

When you open the door to the rest room, you discover four girls from school standing at the mirror and fixing their hair.

(continued on page 11)

"Well, hello," says one of the girls. "Look at you!"

You smile, somewhat shyly. Three of the girls are on the cheerleading squad. The fourth is president of the senior class. They are the core of the in-group at school, and you have never had a conversation with any of them.

"I hardly recognized you. You look terrific," says Debbi, who was in your photography class last year.

"Thanks," you say, unable to come up with anything more interesting.

"Listen," Debbi says as she walks to the door. "Carole here is having a party on Friday night. Why don't you come by?"

You are flattered. They always have big parties that everyone talks about, but you've never been invited to one.

"Great," you say. "I'd love to. But I'd better call you later and let you know for sure. Is it okay if my friend Jill comes with me?"

"Well, I suppose so," Carole says. "I'll write down my address and phone number. Give me a call and I'll fill you in on the details."

"You really do look great," says Debbi as the girls leave.

When you tell Jill the news, she frowns. "Great," she says. "Do you feel important now?"

You are confused. You thought she would love to go. "What's wrong with you?" you say.

(continued on page 12)

"What's wrong with *me?* What's wrong with you? Didn't you ever notice that they never talked to you before? You weren't good enough for them when you were fat. Thank you, but no thank you. I wouldn't be caught dead at one of their parties. They're the kind of people who will use you. If you want to go to the party, it's your decision. But watch out. They'll be your best friends one minute and stab you in the back the next."

You think about what Jill is saying and you know that she is probably right. But you also know that all last year you were on the outside looking in, wanting so much to be a part of the group, a part of their laughter, their fun, their parties. And now you have been invited in.

You know that there's no point in trying to convince Jill to go.

If you go without Jill, turn to page 20.

If you don't go, turn to page 30.

You decide that you'd better not go running around looking for cold cuts. You were hired as a photographer and you'd better do your job.

You are pleased that you made that decision because once the guests begin to arrive, you don't stop for a minute. There are so many mini-dramas to record, so many interesting faces, tender moments. By the time you get home, you are exhausted.

When you pull into your driveway, you notice two guys in your neighbor's side yard.

"Bombs away!" one yells as you get out of your car. Then he dives into a huge pile of leaves from the stone wall that separates the two properties.

As you walk toward your house, you can feel them watching you. You go inside, collapse on your bed, and call Jill. You are explaining how the day went when you hear a noise outside your second-story window. You are too tired to move so you ignore it.

CRASH! You jump up and look out the window. There is a face staring up at you from the ground. An arm waves.

Suddenly you notice a face in the tree, just a few feet from where you are standing.

"Well, hello," this face says. "Do you come here often?"

"You're not going to believe this," you say to Jill.

"Hey," the guy in the tree yells. "Haven't you ever seen a monkey before? I'm a rare breed."

(continued on page 14)

"What's going on over there?!" Jill yells into the phone. You begin to explain, when once again you are interrupted.

"You want to come jump in some leaves?" a voice says. When you look outside this time, there are two pairs of eyes staring at you, making monkey noises. "Come on out and play!"

You laugh. "What's going on?" Jill is yelling in your ear.

The two guys climb down the tree. "Come on down, window woman," they yell when they are on the ground.

When you tell Jill the story, she can't stop laughing.

"Go down," she tells you.

"You think so?" you say.

"Why not?" she says.

If you go outside and meet the monkeys, turn to page 26.

If you decide to stay inside, turn to page 18.

Jill parks her car in front of the gym office.

"Well, hello!" Coach Thomas says when you walk in. "Look at you! You look terrific. I don't think I ought to let those football players anywhere near you."

You laugh, enjoying the compliment.

"You have obviously stopped eating," he says. "You better not come over for dinner anymore. My wife will want to fatten you up."

You remember when you and Jill had dinner at his house last year. His wife made the best lasagna you'd ever had. *No wonder I was so fat,* you think, remembering how much you had eaten.

The coach looks at his watch. "Time for the meeting," he says, and he begins to walk toward the gym. You take a deep breath and follow him. Your legs are shaking and you feel as though you might cave in.

"You're gonna be fine!" Jill whispers; she can always tell what you're thinking.

"Hey, I thought we were having a meeting. Where's the coach?" a voice yells as you approach the gym.

"Right in front of you, Randall," Coach Thomas says as he walks in. "Okay, guys, let's get organized." After a few hoots and howls, everyone sits down.

You are talking to Jill with your back to the group when the coach starts his speech.

"Hey, who's the beauty behind you, Coach?

(continued on page 16)

Aren't we going to be introduced?" calls out a voice.

"Yeah," calls out another. "Let's take care of the important things first."

You can feel your face turn bright red.

"You all know her," says Coach Thomas. "Unless your brains got fried over the summer."

"Wait a minute," says John. "It's the Bobbsey Twins. But check out Bobbsey number two." There are a few whistles and yells.

Your stomach feels as though there are things flying around in it. You've never gotten this kind of attention before. You smile and look at Jill.

"Okay, guys, that's enough," Coach Thomas says. "These two are your managers, so don't mess with them." There is a round of boos and more hooting before the meeting gets under way.

You sit behind the coach taking notes, while Jill goes through the equipment, taking inventory. Throughout the meeting your eyes wander around the room. Many of the guys are staring at you. When your eyes meet theirs, you get waves, winks, smiles. You quickly look away. Even John smiles at you. Your pulse feels as though it's going a million beats a minute. John has never looked cuter. You love the way he uses his fingers to flip his hair off his forehead. Two seconds later it flops down again. It seems that every time you look over at him, he's looking at you.

"Hey, John, I'm talking to you," Coach Thomas

(continued on page 17)

says. "Keep your mind on the game!" The coach looks at you and winks.

The meeting ends with a pep talk and a few hoots and grunts. You and Jill walk toward the door.

"Hey, we're meeting up at the deli in a few minutes, girls. Why don't you join us?" one of the guys yells.

"We'll try," says Jill, smiling at you. "I think you were a hit," she whispers.

As soon as you step out the door, a horn honks. You look over and see Mark, sitting in his blue convertible. His windblown blond hair gives him the look of a truly free spirit; and you had forgotten how wonderful his smile is.

"Hey! Look at you! You look great," he says. "Your mom wasn't kidding when she said I'd be surprised to see you." He jumps out of his car and gives you a big hug. "Long time no see," he says. "Let's go get something to eat."

There has always been a special closeness between you and Mark, and you can't wait to hear about his summer. You know that those blue eyes sparkle especially for you, and you love it. But being invited to go with the football team is new and exciting. John might even be there.

If you tell Mark that you already have plans, turn to page 40.

If you go to lunch with Mark, turn to page 24.

"I am not facing them alone," you say to Jill. "Get over here as fast as you can."

For the next ten minutes you ignore the sounds from the yard next door. There are coyote howls, frog ribbets, and braying donkeys. Finally the noises stop. You peer through a crack in the curtains and see no one.

Two minutes after it quiets down, Jill pulls into your driveway. You go out to meet her. The guys are nowhere in sight.

You and Jill lean against her car and you fill her in on the insanity, detail by detail. You are both laughing when you notice two bushes on the other side of the wall, not more than five feet from where you are standing: a tall bush and a short bush. They were not there ten minutes ago. Through the leafy covering you can easily see the guys standing there, holding branches in front of themselves.

"I think we've been spotted," says one bush.

"I wonder who told," says the other.

"Oh my goodness!" says Jill. "Look at those wilted leaves. Those bushes need watering." She runs for the hose.

"No," screams the big bush. "We're not really bushes. See." They toss away their branches.

"But we are wilted," says the big guy. "You don't happen to have some water in the house, do you?"

"Gee," you say, "we might be out of water. But we do have some apple cider."

"Yahoo," screams the big guy as you all walk into

(continued on page 19)

the kitchen. He turns to his friend. "You owe me ten bucks."

"Curses," says the little guy. "Wrong again."

"What in the world are you two all about?" asks Jill. "You can start by telling us your names."

"I'm Jim," says the one who is well over six feet tall. "And he's Jim. We're identical twins. And we're also the gardeners next door."

"You are out of your heads," you say, pouring the cider. "What's this about ten dollars?"

"Well," says the big Jim, "I bet Jim that before we left today, we could get you to invite us into your house. I won."

You look at Jill. She looks at you. The idea of being the objects of a bet infuriates both of you.

"Out," screams Jill. "You may have been invited in, but your stay is a very short one."

"But we're terrific guys," says the little Jim.

"Sorry," says Jill. "Gambling is illegal." She shoves them out the door.

"They'll be back, you know," you say to Jill after they have left. "I can tell they're the persistent type."

"I know they will," says Jill. "And the truth is that I actually look forward to getting to know them. They're nuts! And probably a lot of fun. But I hope they have learned a lesson."

The End

Later that day, you call Carole and tell her that you will be there. If Jill wants to be stubborn, then that's her problem. The fact is that you really do want to go to that party, even though you are nervous about going alone.

The next day you are shopping at the supermarket when you see Debbi.

"Hi," she says. "Carole told me you're coming to the party. That's great. You'll have a blast!" She has potato chips and soda in her basket.

"Is that for the party?" you ask.

"Sure is. We're going to have a ton of food there. Hey, don't you live over on Elm Street?"

"Yeah," you say.

"Well, I live a block over. If you want, we can drive to Carole's together. That'll save some gas. I have to be there a little early though," she says.

"Great!" you say. "I'll drive." Now you don't have to go alone. Everything is working out perfectly.

At six on Saturday, you pick Debbi up. All the way to Carole's she tells you about the love of her life. She has had a crush on the quarterback, John, for a year, and he is going to be at the party.

When you get to Carole's everyone is really friendly. The whole night goes great; you meet a million new people and the people you know from before are full of compliments about your figure. By the time you leave, you feel on top of the world. Being skinny is the best thing that ever happened to you.

(continued on page 21)

On the way home Debbi tells you about her father, who is a photographer for a top magazine. She knows from class last year that photography is one of your passions.

"Listen," Debbi says, "my dad got me two tickets to the big photography show in New York. Photographers from all around the world are going to be there, and my dad has promised to introduce me to some of them. How would you like to go with me?"

"I'd love to," you say. Meeting all those people and seeing their work would be fantastic! You've never been to anything like that before.

"Great!" Debbi says. "It's Thursday night at five."

You remember that you promised Jill you'd drive to Harvard with her that day. You were going to stay at her grandmother's and come back Friday morning.

If you go to the photography show with Debbi, turn to page 43.

If you go to Harvard with Jill, turn to page 51.

"I'll tell you what," you say. "If you want I can run down to the store and pick up some more meat. You have enough problems."

"Oh, honey, you're a doll!" Mrs. Conroy says. "I'll get some money and give you a list."

You follow her inside, grab a roll of film, and walk to your car. Ricky follows you out.

"I'm parked behind you," he says. "Why don't we just go in my car?"

Whoopee, you think. *Great idea.*

"Okay," you say. Ricky opens the passenger door for you and shuts it when you sit down. He walks around the car to the driver's door. His stride is smooth and confident, his smile is friendly. "I'm Ricky, Mrs. Conroy's nephew," he says as he backs the car out. *He must be a millionaire,* you think. *He couldn't be more than nineteen and look what he's driving.*

"So, how long have you been a photographer?" he asks.

Your hair blows freely as you ride.

"About a year," you say. "I develop my own film and do the printing as well. It's really fun. Tell me something about yourself," you say. *Tell me everything,* you think.

"Well, he says, "I am a senior at Starwell, and I fly planes."

"You fly planes?" you say.

"Yep. I took lessons all last year, and I've been flying all summer."

(continued on page 23)

A Porsche, private school, and a plane; maybe a billionaire. You are so overwhelmed that you have trouble getting words out of your mouth.

"Tell me about your flying," you manage to say. As he talks, you take the cover off your camera and put in the new roll of film. Your case drops on the floor when Ricky comes to a short stop.

"Sorry about that," he says.

"No problem," you say. *Nothing you do could ever be a problem,* you think.

When you arrive back at the house, Ricky hops out of the car and opens your door for you. *It's like out of an old movie,* you think. You step out and then remember that your camera case is still on the floor. As you turn to get it, you realize that if you "accidentally" forgot it, Ricky would have to bring it to your house. *That would be a good way to see him again,* you think.

If you leave the camera case in Ricky's car, turn to page 35.

If you take it with you, turn to page 32.

You decide that you really want to talk to Mark; besides, you don't know what to say to guys you hardly know.

You and Mark go to a salad bar.

"You really look fabulous," says Mark. "I hope you're still the same person you were when you went away."

His blond hair hasn't been cut all summer and you can't decide whether you like it long or not.

"I'm still the same inside," you say.

"Maybe," says Mark. "But people's personalities are affected by what they see in the mirror."

His bangs are definitely too long, you think.

"I brought you a surprise," says Mark. He hands you a big manila envelope.

You open the envelope and your eyes light up. Last spring you fell in love with a horse that lived down the street from you. A beautiful deep-brown filly with a shiny black mane. Mark has created a collage of his photographs of the horse. It is exquisite.

"Oh, Mark, it's beautiful," you say. *I forgot how wonderful he is,* you think.

"I'm glad you like it. Now there's something I have to talk to you about."

"You sound serious," you say.

"I am," says Mark. "It's something I've been thinking about for weeks—even before I knew that you had lost all that weight. As you know, I never cared how much you weighed. As far as I'm concerned, it's what's inside that counts.

(continued on page 25)

"We've been friends for a long time—but when you went away, I realized that I love you."

There are tears in your eyes as Mark speaks. You are afraid to hear what he is going to say next.

He continues. "It's probably not fair, but I know that I'm not going to be able to share you."

You look at Mark—his soft features, his shaggy blond hair, and those intense blue eyes. You have loved him for years, but you are not sure in what way. All you know is that he is very very important to you.

"I'm asking you to go steady," he says.

Your eyes are filled with tears. You want to run around the table and hug him. He is the most considerate person you have ever met in your life.

But all summer, while you were losing weight, while Mark was dreaming about you, you were thinking about how exciting it would be to be thin and attractive . . . and popular. Mark is the only boy you have ever dated. You owe it to yourself to go out with other guys. Of course, you are not certain that others will ask you out. They never have before.

Your head is bouncing back and forth. *Mark is an extraordinary human being,* you think. And you know he likes you for who you are, not for what you look like.

If you say yes to Mark, turn to page 47.

If you say no, turn to page 39.

This should be interesting, you think as you go out the door. You walk to the two-foot-high wall that separates your property from your neighbor's. The two guys are standing side by side. One is very tall and thin, with dark-brown hair and swarthy skin. The other one is short, with sandy-blond hair and fair skin.

"Hi, I'm Jim," the short guy says.

"Hi, I'm Jim," the taller guy says.

"Wait a minute," you say.

"We're twins," the taller guy says. "Identical. Listen, if you have any trouble telling us apart, you can always tell by our rings. Mine's green and Jim's is blue. Oh, by the way, we're the gardeners here, in case you were wondering."

These guys can't be for real, you think. You start to laugh when little Jim stands behind big Jim and moves whenever he does.

"Where are you, you little runt?" big Jim says, turning around. Little Jim stays right behind him, turning at the same time. Then all of a sudden, little Jim runs toward the leaves.

"Last one in is a squashed tomato," he yells. They both bound into the pile at the same time.

"Ouch, you hit my head," a voice yells.

"No, you hit *mine!*" screams another. Both guys come out of the pile holding their heads. You watch the comedy routine until your father gets home. You promised you'd help him cook dinner tonight, so you say goodbye to your newfound crazies.

(continued on page 27)

"Until tomorrow!" little Jim says to you, and he kisses your hand.

The next morning you are awakened by a male voice. "Rapunzel, Rapunzel, throw down your locks," the voice is saying. You roll over and peek out the window. Little Jim is standing below your window, looking up.

"Ahoy, mate," big Jim yells, jumping off the wall. "I've spotted a fair maiden." *These guys are too much,* you think.

It is nine-thirty and you have to meet Jill in one hour. When you leave for her house, you stop to talk to the twins. "Stop drooling all over yourself," big Jim says to little Jim. "She is nice, but you must learn to control yourself like me." You blush and climb into your car.

"I'll see you guys later," you say. The two of them salute you.

When you arrive home at the end of the day, there is a small box on your doorstep with a note. You open the box and a frog jumps in your face. You read the note:

Many good things come in small boxes.
Many other things do too.

Signed,
J & J

The next day, you leave early in the morning to go hiking with Jill. The two musketeers are not there yet. When you arrive home at four-thirty, two

(continued on page 28)

pumpkins are sitting on your doorstep. One is big with star-shaped eyes. The other, smaller one has heart-shaped eyes. You are getting to like all of this attention.

The next day around noon you bring the guys out some lemonade and sit down on the wall.

"She's mine!" little Jim yells.

"No, she's mine!" big Jim yells back.

"Mine!"

"Mine!"

"Let's ask her," little Jim says. "Whose are you?"

You just look at them, dumbfounded. You know that your face is bright red. "I think I hear my mother calling me," you say, and you run into the house.

Even though they are only joking, you really don't want to answer that question. They are both so funny and crazy—and you can't really pick out two separate personalities. They kind of blend into each other. In looks, big Jim is more your type. He has the long, thin, muscular body of a track star, and exquisite coordination. You love to watch him run. He moves so quickly and gracefully.

Little Jim is sort of clumsy and awkward. He reminds you of a puppy dog just learning how to walk; lovable, but not quite together physically.

You are stuck inside doing house chores for the rest of the day, and when you finally go outside, the guys are gone. There is a jar containing four lightning bugs on your doorstep.

(continued on page 29)

The next day when you walk over to say hello, big Jim is sprinkling something on a section of the garden.

"What are you doing?" you ask.

"Sprinkling magic powder on the bushes, of course. They'll have money on them by next week," he says.

You smile. *He's wonderfully wacko,* you think, and you chat with him for a while until you leave to meet Jill.

When you return that night, there is no present, only a note taped to your door. It reads:

> *Roses are red,*
> *Violets are white,*
> *Can I take you to dinner Saturday night?*
> *R.S.V.P.—Blue Ring Jim.*

Blue ring? you think. *That's little Jim, and he's asking for a date.*

You like little Jim, and you know you would have a great time with him; he always makes you laugh. But you know you would never want to be any more than friends with him.

Besides, if you were to go out with little Jim, that could ruin your chances with big Jim. Then again, who knows? Big Jim might never ask you out anyway. And you don't want to hurt little Jim's feelings by saying no.

If you say yes to little Jim, turn to page 45.

If you say no to little Jim, turn to page 36.

Going by yourself into the middle of that group really scares you. You do want to get in with that crowd, but you don't want to start at a big party all by yourself. You are kind of mad at Jill because you know that if she really wanted to go somewhere, you would go with her. And you are angry at yourself for not having the guts to go on your own. But still, you call Carole and tell her that you can't make it.

The next two weeks go by quickly. You go to Boston with Jill for two days, go shopping, and generally keep yourself busy. By the end of the two weeks, you are totally bored with summer and eager to get back to school. You are taking some terrific classes, you are no longer worried about what people are going to say about your weight loss, and you are hoping to move into a whole new social scene.

You are also looking forward to working with Mr. Phillips in Advanced Photography. All last year he kept telling you how talented you were.

On the last day of school he asked you to be his teaching assistant this year. In addition to taking the roll and scheduling the assignments, you will have unlimited darkroom privileges. You can't wait.

When school finally starts, things go just as you had hoped. You are overwhelmed with compliments on your weight loss, and your classes are great. Debbi is in your photography class, along with a lot of good-looking guys. You and she sign up to be partners in your first assignment.

(continued on page 31)

On the third day of school Debbi comes running over to you before lunch.

"Guess what?" she says. "John asked me to go to lunch with him today."

"That's great," you say. Debbi has told you that she's been in love with the football quarterback for a year now.

"But you have to do me a favor," she continues. "I don't want to have to come back for fifth period. John doesn't have any classes after lunch and I don't want to act like the little junior who has to report back to school. When you take the roll in photography, do you think you could put a little check next to my name? Just this one time. It's really important to me."

You suddenly feel trapped. Mr. Phillips has put his trust in you and you really don't want to violate that trust. You know that he probably would never find out, but that isn't the point. You have never had such a good relationship with a teacher before, and you don't want to jeopardize it.

On the other hand, Debbi's friendship has brought you into a whole new circle of friends and you don't want to ruin that either.

If you cover for Debbi, turn to page 65.

If you tell her you can't, turn to page 67.

"Oops," you say. "I forgot my camera case." You reach into the car to pick it up. *I'll probably never see him again,* you think as he walks off to greet a group of relatives.

You don't have time to think about Ricky for the rest of the afternoon. The guests have begun to arrive and you begin shooting.

"Oh, my word, look at you," you hear over and over again. "I can't believe how much you've grown."

"You look great."

"I've missed you."

You try to capture on film the spontaneity and warmth of the greetings. After a summer of shooting nature in New Hampshire, you are delighted to be recording human emotions—smiles, laughter, love, even tears of happiness.

When the initial excitement is over, you concentrate on groups of people interacting. You hate posed pictures where everyone stares at the camera and says "Cheese." Instead, you try to record natural groupings of people enjoying each other. And even some close-ups of interesting faces with your zoom lens.

The very young and the very old have always interested you, and you take one whole roll of children playing, plus half a dozen studies of one old man who seems to be the patriarch of the family. His craggy face reflects his long life, and you hope the camera will record the wisdom in his eyes.

(continued on page 33)

By the end of the afternoon, you are exhausted, but it is an exhilarating exhaustion, one that comes from knowing that you have worked hard and done a good job.

When you drive off, you notice the orange Porsche and you realize that you never did talk to Ricky again. *Oh, well*, you think, *I wasn't there to socialize. I was there to do a job.*

You arrive home, flop down on the floor next to the telephone and call Jill. You have barely begun to tell her about the afternoon when your mother calls you.

"Honey," she begins, and you know that she is about to ask a favor. "I promised Marcy Kaufman that you would drop by with a phone book. They haven't gotten theirs yet, and she needs the Yellow Pages."

"Oh, Mom, do I have to do it now?" you say.

"I'm afraid so," she says. "I was supposed to drop it off this morning. Take your sister with you, because I might have to go out. Oh, and I told Marcy you would take Tommy to school in the morning and help him register."

Ugh. The mention of Tommy Kaufman almost makes you vomit. Marcy is your mother's best friend, and the family used to live next door to you in Michigan when you and Tommy were nine years old. He was the creepiest kid you've ever known. When he wasn't throwing mud at you, he was stealing your toys. And you'll never forget the time he

(continued on page 34)

dumped a jar of green paint on your head. "It'll make you grow faster, Shorty," he yelled and ran away. Fortunately, you moved to Connecticut seven years ago and haven't seen Tommy since. Last week, the Kaufmans moved three blocks away and Tommy is going to be in your class at school.

"Julie," you call to your four-year-old sister. "Let's go." You grab the phone book and climb into the car. Tommy is the last person you want to see. Especially today.

You slow down in front of the Kaufman house and see Tommy shooting baskets in the side yard. You estimate that he must weigh at least 200 pounds. *I can't believe how much you've grown,* you think, your mind echoing the refrain of the afternoon.

You pull up to the next house and tell Julie to drop the phone book on the Kaufmans' front porch. You'll call Marcy later and tell her it's there.

As you drive home, you try to figure out how you can get around having to help Tommy register. The whole idea of your losing all that weight and then having to walk into school on the first day with that obnoxious blimp is too much! You have already registered for your classes, but you know that your friend Jill has to register tomorrow morning.

If you try to convince Jill to take Tommy with her, turn to page 52.

If you make arrangements to take Tommy yourself, turn to page 55.

You cross your fingers and "forget" your case.

The rest of the party goes well and you get some great shots; but you only get to talk to Ricky once. You are too busy shooting. As you drive home, you decide that you will probably never see him or your camera case again.

For the next two days, you develop the film, make contact sheets, and print a few of your favorite shots. Sunday night you are trying to organize the negatives, but your little sister, Julie, keeps coming into your room and bothering you. Finally you send her to watch TV.

"You look like a polka-dotted monster," she shouts at you and runs off.

You look in the mirror and laugh at yourself. Your bangs are pinned up, your hair is in clips, and you have little dots of zit cream all over your face. You actually do resemble a monster.

At eight o'clock your mom and dad leave for a party. "Sue is coming by with a package for me," says your mom. "Keep your music low so you'll hear the bell."

A half hour later the doorbell rings. "Julie, get the door," you yell.

"I can't. I'm watching TV," she answers.

If you answer the door, turn to page 88.

If you make Julie get it, turn to page 94.

You decide that it wouldn't be fair to lead little Jim on. You figure he probably has more in mind than just friendship. So you spend the evening trying to figure out the gentlest way to say no. You end up deciding to use a classic excuse. You hope that he gets the message.

The next morning, before the Jims arrive, you spear a note for little Jim onto their pitchfork.

> To Blue Ring Jim:
>   I'm happy to learn
>   That violets are white
>   But I have to babysit
>   Saturday night
>   Sorry.

Then you take off for Jill's, hoping to avoid seeing little Jim. You know that little Jim doesn't work the next day, and by two days from now, he'll probably have forgotten the whole thing.

When you get home at five, the guys are not there. You sigh in relief. *I made it through the day,* you think. As you are chopping a cucumber for your salad, you think about big Jim. You didn't accept the date with little Jim mostly because you would like to go out with big Jim. *So now what do I do?* you wonder. *Probably I'll have to make the first move,* you think.

You decide that since little Jim doesn't work tomorrow, that will be your best chance to flirt with

(continued on page 37)

big Jim. *I'll have him all to myself*, you think. You laugh when you think about big Jim putting magic powder on his plants to grow money.

That's it, you think. *What would big Jim do if he came to work tomorrow and found money growing on his bushes. He would love it!* you decide.

You run around the house collecting every penny, dime, and nickel you can find. Then you take a roll of tape and go outside. You tape the coins all over the bushes in the magic patch. You can't stop giggling as you work, and all night you keep wondering what big Jim's reaction is going to be. You have never done anything quite so silly before, and you are secretly proud of your courage and imagination.

The next morning you get up early and peek out the window. There is no sign of big Jim. It isn't until ten o'clock that you hear his truck pull up. You run to your window and peek out through the curtains. You watch impatiently as he rakes the leaves and packs them into plastic bags. You watch as he trims some hedges. He does some planting on the other side of the yard. And then, finally, he takes the hose and moves toward the money bushes. You watch a smile grow on his face as he bends over the plants. He looks up toward your window, and you jump back.

You sit around the house all day, waiting for some reaction, but there is nothing! No pebbles at the window, no coyote yells, no screaming. At four-

(continued on page 38)

thirty you hear Jim's truck start, then he disappears.

Great, you think. *That brilliant idea sure did a lot of good. I think I made a fool of myself.* You go downstairs and put some popcorn in your air popper.

About ten minutes later the doorbell rings. When you open the door, big Jim is standing before you with a red rose in his hand.

"Guess what?" he says, handing you the rose. "My magic worked! My tree grew money. How would you like to go to dinner? I'm rich now." You can't keep from smiling.

"I'd love to," you say.

Who ever said there's no such thing as magic?

The End

It would be so easy and comfortable to go steady with Mark, but you know that you owe it to yourself to meet new people, have new experiences. You hope Mark will continue to be a part of your life, but you just won't go steady and close everyone else out. When you explain your feelings to Mark, he doesn't seem surprised.

"I had a feeling that was going to be your answer. I'm disappointed, but I understand," Mark says in a soft voice.

When he drops you off at your house and says goodbye, you feel an emptiness in your heart. You walk into the kitchen and are about to take a pint of ice cream out of the freezer. *No,* you say to yourself. *That's the old me. Eating doesn't solve problems; it creates them.* You slam the freezer door.

There is a note on the counter for you. The man in charge of the county fair has called to see if you want to work one of the booths again this year. You are thrilled with the offer; it will take your mind off Mark. You call back and accept the job of working a baseball-throw game booth.

Turn to page 60.

You swallow hard, not sure if you like what you are about to do.

"Listen," you say to Mark, "I've already made plans, but why don't you come over tonight?"

His smile shrinks. "Okay," he says, disappointed. "Around seven?"

"That'll be great!" you say and give him another hug. "See you then."

You and Jill wait until Mark has driven off before you get into her car and drive to the deli. You both walk slowly toward the entrance.

"You go first," Jill says to you.

"No way. You go first," you say.

Both of you pull the door open and you walk in together. Someone whistles from across the room. You and Jill see a table in the back filled with guys.

"Come on back, girls," a voice yells. You turn to Jill and start to laugh. She laughs too. You and she have always used laughter to get you through tough situations. Whenever you find yourselves laughing in inappropriate situations, you know you're nervous! *What in the world are we going to talk about?* you wonder as you walk back.

"Hey, come sit here," calls John, as he dumps one of the guys off the chair next to him. "Touchdown," he yells, pretending that the fellow on the floor has been tackled. Then John holds his hands out to catch an imaginary pass. "And we're in. We've done it again! That's what this season's all about. Right, guys?"

(continued on page 41)

"Right," says Joe, a tall, muscular blond. "With my speed, your passes, and the rest of these turkeys to back us up, we're in there for the championship."

"Hey, you forgot two people," John says, turning toward you and Jill. "We've got our managers here. Whenever we're in trouble, we'll just look over at them for inspiration."

He turns to you and smiles. You look into his sparkling chocolate-brown eyes and feel yourself sinking right through your seat.

"Guess what, guys," John says. "You all get to listen to my sexy voice on the PA this year. I'm going to be doing the morning announcements. Ha! They don't know what they're getting themselves into. Give me some power, and next thing you know I'll be taking over!" he says, laughing.

He's got everything going for him, you think. *Grades, talent, power, and looks.* You can't stop staring at him. He's like a magnet. And, of course, he knows it.

When the group breaks up, everyone heads home. As you and Jill walk toward her car, someone pulls on the back of your hair. You turn around and stare at a chin. When you look up, you are staring into those deep, dark eyes again.

John puts his hand on your shoulder. You feel a tingling sensation down your arm.

"Listen," he says. "A bunch of people are playing miniature golf tonight. I get off work at half past nine. Do you want to go?"

(continued on page 42)

You cannot believe that he is asking you out. The number-one catch in the school is asking you for a date!

Then suddenly you remember that you have asked Mark to come over at seven. In a matter of seconds, your head spins in a million different directions. You know you would have to lie to Mark about why he had to leave by nine-thirty. And you hate to do that. But you *would* have two and a half hours together; it isn't as though you are canceling out on him. Besides, you and Mark aren't going steady or anything like that. You're entitled to have other dates. How can you say no to the most popular guy in the school? How could anybody? Your mind is made up.

You have no choice.
Turn to page 48.

You decide that you and Jill can go to Harvard some other weekend. It isn't only the show; it's also the idea of being included in the in-group. You have been "out" for so long; now that you are being included, you really don't want to say no to any invitations that come your way.

Jill is furious when you tell her that you can't go. You knew she would be upset, but you also know that she'll forgive you. You've been friends for too long for this to seriously affect your friendship. You can't help feeling terrible, though.

Jill barely talks to you all week. When you call, she's never there. And she doesn't call you back. You really don't have time to worry about it. You are too busy thinking about and planning for the photography show.

On Wednesday afternoon you go shopping for something special to wear. You even stop at the makeup counter in the department store and get advice on what makeup to wear with your new outfit.

When you return from shopping, there is a note for you to call Debbi.

"I have bad news," she says. "Well—bad and good. I was talking to John yesterday and I told him about the show. You'll never guess what he said? He said he wanted to go with me. Can you believe that? He isn't even interested in photography. I'm sure he wants to go just to be with me! Naturally, I couldn't say no to him. I knew you'd understand."

(continued on page 44)

You are speechless. You've been looking forward to this all week.

"Sorry," Debbi says. "Listen, I've got to go figure out a whole new outfit to wear. I'll call you later, okay?"

You hang up the phone and just sit there. *Doesn't she understand how important that was to me?* you think. *What kind of friend would . . . ?*

You stop your thought in the middle. That's exactly what you just did to Jill. Going to Harvard was as important to her as this was to you. Suddenly you realize that you hurt Jill the same way Debbi just hurt you. You never would have done that to your friend last year. *Losing weight has warped my mind,* you think, as you pick up the phone to call Jill.

The End

The next morning little Jim's face lights up when you tell him yes. After you leave him, he bounds back to big Jim with the news.

When you go to the store later that day, big Jim comes over to you as you are getting into the car.

"You know," he says, "that's a good man over there."

You smile half-heartedly. *But you're a better man,* you think. Now you are not sure you made the right decision. When you look at big Jim, something happens to you. Your heartbeat speeds up and you get a funny tingling feeling in your stomach. When you look at little Jim, nothing happens. *Oh, well,* you think, *too late now.*

On Saturday night you throw on a pair of gray pants and a black shirt. You are not very excited about the date and you don't feel like fussing with clothes. *At least I'll be entertained,* you think.

Little Jim arrives at six and you drive to an Italian restaurant in Westport. He doesn't say very much, and you feel as though you are riding with someone you have never met before. At dinner you talk about school, your families, your jobs. Conversation is difficult and strained. You feel the way you sometimes do with your parents' friends. You only laugh once the whole night, and that is when your waiter trips and spills cocktail sauce all over a bald man's head.

There are many awkward moments when you and Jim are silent. You try to think of things to say, but

(continued on page 46)

all you can think about is going home. You wish you had never said yes to this date. Little Jim is not the same; he is only half a person. His humorous, crazy side is lost without big Jim.

When you finally go home, you thank little Jim and quickly go inside. The last thing you want to do is give him a goodnight kiss. You lie in bed and think about what a horrible evening it was. *Not only was the night boring,* you think, *but I have ruined my chances with big Jim.*

Better luck next time.

The End

"Oh, Mark. You make me feel so special. You are more important to me than any other person in my whole life," you say, tears streaming down your cheeks. "I think going steady is a great idea. I would love to."

You look at Mark as you speak. He is glowing. The smile on his face would brighten a midnight sky.

"Let's get out of here," he says, taking your hand and squeezing it. He starts to run when you get out the door.

"I'm so happy I don't know how to tell you," he says as you get into the car.

He is quiet as he drives to Overlook Pass just outside of town. Then he stops the car and runs to the top of the hill that looks over miles of countryside. You run after him. By the time you reach the top of the hill, Mark's hands are cupped around his mouth and he is shouting. "Hey, world. We're going steady." Then he turns to you. First he kisses you gently on your forehead. Then your nose. Then he takes you in his arms and presses his lips to yours. You can feel his love in every inch of your body. You can feel his strength, his caring, his passion. You have never been so happy in your life.

The End

I'm sure I can work it out, you think, trembling a little. Then you tell John, "I love miniature golf. I'd be glad to go with you."

"Terrific," says John. "See you later."

"Oh, Jill," you say when you get into the car. "What am I going to do? Mark is due at seven and John is coming at nine-forty."

"Not bad," says Jill. "Did you ever think you'd be complaining about having too many dates? You'll just have to get Mark out by half past nine."

"I hate doing that to Mark," you say. "But how can I say no to the most popular guy in school?"

"I don't know," says Jill. "But be careful."

That night, Mark arrives at seven. After two hours of stories, gossip, and catching up, you tell Mark that you aren't feeling well and that you'd better make it an early evening. A half hour later, he leaves, promising to call in the morning to make sure you're all right. You feel like a rat.

It is nine-thirty-five when Mark walks out the door. John arrives only five minutes later.

At the golf range you meet a bunch of the football players and their girlfriends. Everyone treats you as though you've been friends with them for years. When you make two holes-in-one in a row, everyone cheers.

"You don't think that I would pick an uncoordinated girl, do you?" John says. "I only choose the best." He gives you a hug.

(continued on page 49)

When John takes you home, he tells you that he approves of the new you and that he's glad he met you before you were mobbed by all the guys. John makes you feel like a prize, a princess, a star. And you love it!

For the next two weeks, you manage to date both Mark and John. Luckily, John is busy at football when Mark is free; and Mark is taking yearbook shots when John is free. And by some incredible miracle, they have jobs on different nights.

As each day passes, you grow more and more confused. You like them both in different ways: Mark for the warmth and closeness; John for the excitement.

Trouble soon comes your way, though. On Friday, Mark asks you to the Homecoming Dance. You change the subject and disappear.

When you pick up John from practice that afternoon, he greets you with, "Hey, cutie, what color dress are you going to wear to the dance next week? I want us to look like the perfect couple."

Just what you needed to hear!

That night you really want to bury your problems in a hot fudge sundae. You settle instead for a bowl of butterless popcorn.

As you devour the popcorn, you try to get your head together. Mark is the most considerate person you have ever known. He is smart and talented and sensitive to your needs, and he is always full of

(continued on page 50)

wonderful surprises. But most of all, you know that he likes you for what you are, not for what you look like. When you are with Mark, you feel comfortable, relaxed, and secure.

John, on the other hand, is exciting. When you are with him, your blood flows faster, your heart beats louder, and besides, he has been wonderful to you these past two weeks. To go to Homecoming with the school quarterback is like a dream come true.

You cannot stand having to make this decision. Maybe you should get sick. Then you wouldn't have to say no to anyone.

If you go with John, turn to page 57.

If you go with Mark, turn to page 68.

If you get sick, turn to page 63.

"I can't go," you say. "I already have plans."

"Oh, well. It would have been fun," Debbi says.

When you get home, you sit on your bed and think about what you just did. *I guess that's what friends are for,* you think.

Thursday morning, Jill picks you up. The first part of the drive is strange; Jill barely talks to you. You have never seen her so quiet.

"What's wrong?" you say. At first she shrugs her shoulders; then she bursts into tears.

"My parents are getting a divorce," she says.

Jill told you that they'd been fighting, but this is the first time she's mentioned divorce.

"I'm so glad you came with me today," Jill says. "I really need to talk to you."

You spend most of the drive talking about divorce. It's the first time Jill has allowed her feelings to surface; her fears, her anger, her feelings of guilt tumble out in words and tears.

By the time you get to Harvard, Jill is feeling better for having opened up with all the things she's kept locked up for more than a month.

When Jill drops you off at home the next day, she hugs you, "Thanks for everything," she says. "I don't know what I would do without you."

You feel proud that you were there when Jill needed you.

The End

You and Jill have been friends since fourth grade, when her house burned down and her family lived with yours for two months. In fifth grade, you gave her the mumps and then sat in her room and played games with her for a whole week in the middle of the summer. In sixth grade you made a blood pact by pricking your thumbs, mixing your blood, and promising to be best friends forever. *Well,* you think as you dial her number, *this is it. The true test of our friendship.*

"Hey, look," Jill says when you ask her to take Tommy with her to school. "It's not such a big deal for me. I mean, he never dumped paint on *my* hair. But I promised my mom for the fifth day in a row that I would clean my room. If I don't do it tomorrow morning, I'm grounded for the weekend.

"Jill, darling," you say, smelling success and happy to pay for it, "while you introduce Tommy to Bridgeport's finest high school, I and twenty of my trusted elves will make your room sparkle as it has never sparkled before. Every penguin in your collection will be personally bathed and polished. Your sticky door handle will gleam. And the thousands of fingerprints on your walls, half of which are mine, will disappear in a poof of Fantastic."

"I think I'm the winner in this deal," says Jill.

"Jill, believe me, no amount of hard labor could equal five minutes with Tommy. Thanks a bunch. I love you."

At quarter to nine the next morning you arrive at Jill's with sponges, furniture oil, rags, and an as-

(continued on page 53)

sortment of liquid cleaners. Jill greets you at the door. She looks fabulous in a vivid blue blouse that matches her blue eyes, and black shorts that make her black hair look like part of her outfit. *What a waste*, you think. *All that beauty used up on a creep like Tommy*.

"Thanks," you yell as she pulls out of the driveway.

"Hey, don't thank me. I still think I'm getting the best part of this deal."

"Tell me that *after* you meet Tommy," you say, feeling guilty for sending your best friend off with a guy who once put a dead cat on your front doorstep.

Jill's room, as usual, looks "lived in." You start by folding up the clothes that are in piles all over the floor. Some of them are sandy from the beach; those go into the hamper. So do the ones that smell of suntan lotion. Most of the others are clean; you put them into her dresser drawers or on hangers in the closet.

Under the clothes is a pile of your letters from New Hampshire, a final exam from history class, gum wrappers, four mystery books, and your green sweatshirt that has been missing since May.

When the floor is clean, you empty all the shelves onto the bed. Jill is a collector of figurines. Besides penguins, she has millions of tiny owls. One by one, you dust them and put them back on the shelves.

By eleven the fingerprints are gone from the walls.

You drive home and curl up in the living room

(continued on page 54)

with *Gone with the Wind*. An hour later, as you are panting over Rhett Butler, the doorbell rings. You open the door and see Jill, her blue eyes sparkling. She is holding the hand of a six-foot-tall guy with curly blond hair.

Where in the world did this incredible hunk of a man come from? you wonder. And then he smiles. The body is different; the face is different; even the hair is different. But you would recognize the smile anywhere. It's the smile of a nine-year-old when he puts a spider on your leg; the smile of a boy who is sneaking your favorite toy into his wagon; the smile of a monster when he watches your reaction to a dead cat. In a nine-year-old it was obnoxious. In a six-foot-tall sixteen-year-old, that spark of mischief in his smile is irresistible.

"Surprise," says Jill. "Meet Tommy. Old friend, new image."

"That was my cousin you saw in the driveway," says Tommy. "Sorry about the mix-up."

You can tell by the look on Jill's face that she is deliriously happy. *Who wouldn't be with a hunk like that?* you think.

The End

At nine the next morning you pull into the Kaufman driveway.

A basketball rolls toward the car; then Tommy rolls over to pick it up.

"Just a minute," he calls and goes into the house. *If he brings out a dead cat I'll drive away,* you think. You put your feet up on the passenger seat and lean against your door.

"Hey, Shorty," a deep voice calls from behind you. *That's it,* you think. *He still acts like a nine-year-old.*

When you turn around, you are facing a tall, handsome guy with curly hair. Following close behind is Tommy.

"Aren't you going to say hi to me?" the tall blond says.

"Well, hi," you say, trying to figure out if you've ever met him before.

"This is my cousin, Robert," the good-looking boy says, pointing to the basketball boy. You are confused.

"Nice to meet you," you say, suddenly smiling. You were all wrong. *It's his cousin!* you think, laughing to yourself.

"Ready to go?" the real Tommy says.

"Sure am," you say. "Hop in." As you pull away, you both wave to Robert.

"Well," you say, "you've definitely changed."

"Well, I was nine years old the last time you saw me," he says, smiling. *He still has that mischievous*

(continued on page 56)

grin and those devious green eyes, you think. *But now they look great.*

When you get to school, you show Tommy around and help him choose his classes. All of the cheerleaders are standing in one corner of the gym when you walk in with Tommy. Every head turns.

"Hi, how are you!" Suzie, the head cheerleader yells to you. She's never talked to you before. *She probably doesn't even know my name,* you think.

"Fine, thanks," you say. You take Tommy's hand and begin to walk out. You know that the whole group in the corner is watching you, and you love it!

"Aren't you going to introduce me?" asks Tommy.

You are torn. On one hand, you would like Tommy to think that you are part of the popular crowd. You know that if you walk over there with him it will look as though you are friendly with these girls.

On the other hand, it's rather nice to have Tommy all to yourself, to have *them* envious of *you* for a change.

If you introduce him, turn to page 81.

If you don't, turn to page 74.

That night, instead of waiting for Mark to call you, you call him. "Mark," you say over the phone, "I have been invited to Homecoming by John Montgomery and I've decided to go with him." You wait for a reaction, but there is only silence.

"Oh, Mark, I feel awful doing this to you. I really do care for you. A lot. Please don't hate me." There is still no reaction.

"Mark? Please say something."

"There's not much to say." You can hear the coldness in his voice, and you feel the tears in your eyes. "I'll see you around, I guess," he says and hangs up.

You know that he'll get over it, and the two of you can still be friends. But you feel sad anyway.

The next day Jill calls you at about five. "Listen," she says, "Mark asked me to the dance. I wanted to check with you before I gave him an answer. It would just be as friends, and I think he needs a friend really bad."

You know you can't say no, but something inside of you wants to. You shouldn't be jealous, but you can't help yourself.

"Go ahead," you say. "I'm sure you'll have a good time. I gotta go; dinner's ready." You are still sitting by the phone when the doorbell rings.

"Hi, beautiful!" John says when you open the door. He pulls a red rose from behind his back and hands it to you. "Just thought I would stop by to say hello on my way home. I'll call you later." He gives you a hug and trots off to his car.

(continued on page 58)

Holding the rose to your nose, you watch him drive away. The fragrance changes your mood, and you feel a smile begin. You know you have made the right decision.

From that moment on, everything is perfect. John is the star of the homecoming game; he completes seventeen out of seventeen passes. When the game is finished, as the crowd cheers him, he runs over to you on the sidelines and swings you up in the air. "You're my good-luck charm," he says. "And I'm not letting you go!" You are floating.

When he arrives that night to pick you up for the dance, he hands you a corsage of tiny red roses and baby's breath. "You look beautiful," he whispers. You can feel a tingling in your whole body as you walk to the car with your arms around each other.

You practically bounce into the dance. Heads turn as you and John greet everyone.

"You two are just the cutest couple," Suzie, the head cheerleader, says. "You'd think you've been together for years." John squeezes your hand and you both smile.

When John introduces the Homecoming Queen and her court, he insists that you stand by his side. "You're my moral support," he says. "I need you next to me."

You stare at the crowd, then at John. *This is really happening to me,* you think. *I am standing on stage with the star of the school.* You can't believe it. When the announcements are finished, you walk

(continued on page 59)

back to your table. "You're prettier than any of the winners," John whispers to you.

When John takes you home, you stand on the porch for a moment, holding hands. The moon is full, the sky is clear, and the stars have never looked so beautiful. John puts his arms around you and brings his lips to yours. You feel as though you are ten feet off the ground. You wish you could hold the moment forever.

"Thanks," he says. "It was wonderful. I'll call you in the morning." He kisses you once more and walks to his car. You stand there until he has driven away. Then you float into the house.

The End

The next day you pull into the parking lot at the fair. The first person you see is a schoolmate named Chris. Ever since sixth grade Chris has made nasty comments about your weight. He is a class-A creep. Unfortunately, he is also very good-looking. He has dark-brown hair and big brown eyes and half the girls in the school are crazy about him. As far as you are concerned, his eyes are beady, his hair looks like a mop, and he bears a very strong resemblance to a bug.

"Well, well, well. Look who's here," he says, walking over to you with three other guys. "You seem to have gone through a few changes. Now all you need is a chest and maybe we could get together sometime." The guys laugh.

"Some other century, Chris," you say. You turn your back on him and walk away. There are tears in your eyes.

"Well, I guess your fat head hasn't gotten any thinner," he says. You would like to bash in *his* fat head.

When you reach the baseball-throw booth, there is a scrawny redheaded boy behind the counter. "Hey, how 'bout giving this a try?" he calls.

"I'm working here," you say.

"That's funny, I'm the one behind the counter, not you." He laughs.

You aren't quite sure what was so funny, but you shrug it off and enter the booth. "Baseball is for boys. Shouldn't you be working with dolls or something?" he says, laughing again.

(continued on page 61)

Wonderful morning this is, you think.

"Well," he continues, "if we have to work together, I better teach you how to run this game."

Who does this runt think he is? you think. "Don't bother, I've worked here before," you say. He ignores you.

"You just take one of the baseballs and try to knock over the stuffed rabbits. We can set up the animals by stepping on this pedal," he says.

You put your things away and begin to arrange the prizes.

"Hey, you better listen, I don't want you to mess up," he continues.

"I know how to run the place," you say. You are still burning up from Chris's comments and don't feel like dealing with this freckle-faced twerp.

"Oh, by the way," he says, "I'm Ron." *Figures,* you think. *Jill's dog is named Ron.*

You finish organizing the prizes and walk to the front of the stand. Directly across from your booth are the roller coaster and the haunted house.

While you are surveying the area, you notice that a tall blond guy in shorts, who obviously works at the fair, keeps walking back and forth. He waves to you and smiles every time he walks by, but he never comes over.

The other interesting sight is the sandy-haired male collecting tickets for the roller coaster. He is wearing a straw hat and from where you are standing, he looks like a young Paul Newman. *Too bad I hate roller coasters,* you think.

(continued on page 62)

"Hello," a voice says to you. A short woman with a red-and-blue scarf on her head is standing before your booth. "I'm Anitra. I tell fortunes next door."

"Hi, neighbor," you say.

"I just came by to introduce myself. If you would like to come and have your fortune told, I will do it for free."

"Thanks," you say. She's the first nice person you've talked to all morning.

The morning is slow, but gradually, the crowds pile in. After three hours of work, you have $32.50 in your money box; and Ron is still driving you up the wall. He keeps racing you to the customers so that he can collect the money for *his* box. As if you are in competition! Finally you tell him that you are taking a break.

If you go to have your fortune told, turn to page 83.

If you decide to try the Haunted House, turn to page 72.

On Thursday you stay home from school. Even your mother is convinced that you have the flu.

That night you call Mark and John and explain that you are too sick to go to the dance. Mark says that he'll come over Friday to see how you are. John is very disappointed that you can't go, but he explains that as quarterback of the football team, he is obligated to go to the dance. He tells you that he is going to invite Debbi, one of the cheerleaders.

Friday night is horrible. You sit home feeling sorry for yourself. Mark comes over to cheer you up. He tells you that he has something really special planned for next Saturday night. He knows how much this dance meant to you, so he wants to do something wonderful to take its place.

"It's a surprise," he says, with a gleam in his eyes.

Listening to Mark only makes you feel more and more guilty because you can't keep your mind off John. He is at the dance with Debbi. Everyone is in love with cute, bouncy Debbi; so why does she have to like John?

The next morning you call John. You know that you've hurt his ego by not going to the dance, and you are going to have to make the next move.

"I'm really sorry about the dance," you say. "I'd like to make it up to you. Let me take you out to dinner for your birthday next Friday night."

"Great!" John says. "It's a deal." You know that he is happy because his voice always goes up when he is excited. "But can we make it Saturday night? I

(continued on page 64)

always go out to dinner with my parents on the day of my birthday."

Saturday, you think. *Mark has made plans for that night.*

But it's the only day you can go out with John. You can't celebrate his birthday a week late, and you aren't allowed to go out on weeknights.

If you cancel Mark and take John out, turn to page 70.

If you tell John that you have plans for Saturday, turn to page 82.

"Okay," you say, "I'll check you in, but don't let Mr. Phillips see you."

"Thanks," Debbi says and hugs you. "You're a sweetheart!" She bounces off.

In class, you check off her name as if she is there. You know that there is no way Mr. Phillips will ever find out but there is a sick feeling in your stomach. You feel as though you are letting him down.

Two days later Debbi asks you to do it again. This time she wants to go buy a new outfit for that night and she won't have time to shop if she comes to class. Reluctantly you agree once again.

You are troubled by what you are doing. Obviously this is only the beginning of a pattern. You can see her asking you for favors all year long.

You don't want to have to say no to Debbi, but you don't want to cheat on Mr. Phillips either. You spend all weekend searching for a solution.

On Monday you tell Mr. Phillips that you are going to have to give up the job of teaching assistant. You tell him that it is taking away from your work time and you are falling behind in class. He is understanding and agrees to do the job himself. He has no idea what your real reason is; his only concern is that you do well in the class.

On Tuesday Debbi invites you to a party her friend is having. "We can go together," she says. "There's going to be a live band. It'll be great."

You cannot quite believe how friendly Debbi is toward you. Knowing her has automatically whirled you into her very active social life and you love it!

(continued on page 66)

On Wednesday Debbi asks you to mark her "present" again. You explain that you're not taking the roll anymore, that you had to give up the job. She tilts her head and looks at you funny.

"When did this come about?" she asks.

"Yesterday," you answer. "Mr. Phillips decided to take the roll himself." You can tell that Debbi doesn't believe you.

"Yeah, well, thanks anyway," she says and walks off.

That weekend you go to the party with her, but she isn't the same. She walks off when you get there, and she barely talks to you all night. In school a few days later she excuses herself when you join her at lunch.

As you watch her walk off with her tray, leaving you alone at the table, Jill's words echo in your head. "The kind of people who will use you," she had said. You should have listened to her.

The End

"I really can't," you say to Debbi.

"What's the big deal?"

"I just can't do it," you repeat.

"I should have figured," she says and walks off. After a few steps, she turns around. "Oh, by the way, that party I told you about? It's canceled."

You can feel the stab in your back. *Jill was right*, you think. *I don't need friends like Debbi.*

The End

You and Mark have gone to every dance together since you met. There's no way you can say no to him. You call John and tell him the bad news.

"Hey, it's your loss," he says and he hangs up. You know that everything between you and John is over.

When you talk to Mark, he is so excited that you almost forget about John. *John was too conceited anyway,* you tell yourself.

Saturday night Mark rings the bell at eight sharp. When you open the door, he hands you a beautiful orchid corsage. When you look at his radiant smile, you are glad you decided to go with him. You feel so close to him and so comfortable.

At the dance, however, something new and different happens. People keep cutting in. Guys keep coming over and asking you to dance. They all keep telling you how fantastic you look. You can't believe the attention you are getting. It is all so new and exciting. You barely dance with Mark all night.

When it's time to leave, you and Mark walk to his car. "This has been a very difficult night for me," he says. "I started out thinking I was going to ask you to go steady. And I've ended up realizing that I can't."

You don't know what to say.

"There is suddenly a new world out there for you, and I care for you too much to keep you away from it. You owe it to yourself to have new experiences, to take advantage of your new popularity. As much

(continued on page 69)

as I want to, I know that it wouldn't be fair to lock you up."

As you look into his eyes, you wipe a tear from your cheek. You can see tears in his eyes, too.

"I still want to see you," you say.

"And I want to see you. But maybe not so much," he says.

You know that he is right. You do need time to get to know the new you. You cannot hide in this comfortable relationship of the past. You owe it to yourself to expand, meet new people, date others.

"Okay," you say and give him a hug.

When he drops you off, you look into his eyes. "I'll see ya," he says, and he walks quickly to his car. You're on your own now. Skinny and free. So why are you crying!

The End

You tell Mark that you have to go to an anniversary party for your aunt Saturday night.

"So much for my surprise," he says. When you look at his big hazel eyes, you can see the tears welling up in them. "We'll make it another time."

You feel a lump in your throat. You hate hurting Mark. He is one of the most important people in your life. It's too late now, though; you have to plan your date with John. You make reservations at Maria's, the best Italian restaurant in town.

Saturday night you pick John up and drive to the restaurant. John is wearing gray slacks, a light-blue shirt, and a navy blazer. His tie is maroon and navy. His broad shoulders fill the jacket perfectly and he looks handsomer than ever before. You are wearing a navy-and-white dress, and you look stunning together.

Over dinner, you talk about how lucky you are to have met. John is in a great mood and the two of you spend most of dinner looking into each other's eyes and smiling. Toward the end of dinner, the subject of going steady comes up.

John says that he feels he is too young to make any commitments. He wants to date you, but he feels that you should both have the freedom to date others.

Now everything is even better than perfect. You have just been given permission to date Mark. There won't have to be any more sneaking around.

(continued on page 71)

You know John cares about you, and now you will be able to have everything.

You are looking at the dessert menu when the waiter walks over, carrying a slice of cheesecake and a piece of paper.

"A complimentary dessert from the gentleman at the first table," the waiter says as he hands you a note. You look across the restaurant to see Mark with an unfamiliar man. For a moment your eyes meet.

Your hands are shaking as you open the note: *I guess the surprise is on me—Mark.*

The End

You walk toward the Haunted House. It looks like a house you might see in a horror movie, with a drawbridge and a pointed roof. There are lights flashing through the dark windows and eyes staring from within. Rattling chains, screeches, and howling noises emanate from the front door.

You show your employee pass and walk in. At first you find yourself in a pitch-black corridor, surrounded by the laughter and screeching of unknown creatures. Then you enter a dimly lit room, filled with coffins. As you cross the room, something jumps out of one of the coffins and grabs your arm. You scream and run forward.

The next dark chamber you come to is filled with spiderwebs; rats are scurrying around your feet. *I'm sure they're fake,* you think. *But they sure look real.*

Suddenly something moves in front of you. You jump back. Then two furry arms grab you from behind, lift you up, and carry you forward. You are screaming and squirming as this creature takes you through the house. A spider drops on your arm. Howls and crazed laughter surround you.

A door flies open and a skeleton falls out. And all this time you are in the furry clutches of some creature that you cannot see. You try to scream, but nothing comes out.

Next you are carried into a dark room where thousands of shining eyes stare at you.

Then, finally, you enter a lighted room. You turn to look at the animal that has been carrying you. It

(continued on page 73)

has fur all over its body and a grotesque face, full of fur and warts. This werewolf carries you outside and puts you down. You are breathing fast and are relieved to be in natural light.

"Before I reveal myself," this creature says to you, "you must answer a question."

"What are you talking about?" you say, looking at this hairy horror.

"Will you come to lunch with me?" the thing says.

You start to laugh when you realize you are having a conversation with a werewolf.

"It's not funny," he says. "What is your answer?"

How can I keep from laughing? you wonder. *And who is under that mask? What weirdo would choose to hide inside a werewolf costume?*

"Who are you?" you ask.

"You will never know unless you agree to have lunch with me," says the beast. "I only like women who take risks."

If you accept his invitation, turn to page 103.

If you say no, turn to page 100.

"I promised to have the car back by noon," you say. "We're already pushing it. Is it all right if we save it for next time?"

"No problem," says Tommy. "I really appreciate your helping me out this morning. I promise that I will never again put a dead cat outside your door." He laughs. You love the way his eyes crinkle.

As you walk to the car, you notice that the blond curls you used to find so obnoxious now look soft and sexy. The squeaky voice that used to yell nasty things at you has become deep and mysterious. And to top it off, Tommy is an intelligent and amusing companion.

When you get home, you call Jill.

"So he turned out great," she says. "Maybe it was predestined."

"I hope so," you say. "At this point, though, I'm afraid we're just family friends. I don't have a clue as to how to switch from family friend to girlfriend. Maybe we're predestined to be pals forever."

"Just let it happen," says Jill. "Don't try to push anything."

As soon as you hang up the phone, your mom walks into the room and tells you not to make plans for tomorrow night. Your family is going out to dinner with the Kaufmans. *Family friend,* you think. But you are happy for the chance to see him again.

The next night you wear your bright blue skirt with a blue-and-black top and black shoes. Jill says the outfit makes you look sexy.

(continued on page 75)

At five minutes to six your dad parks next to a movie theater that is showing *Star Wars*. Two minutes later, the Kaufmans pull up behind you. Tommy catches up to you as you walk down the block to the Chinese restaurant. He is wearing a green shirt that matches his eyes. *Is it possible to flirt in front of your parents?* you wonder. *A little awkward,* you think, *but I'll be subtle.*

When you get to the table, you try to figure out how you can get to sit next to Tommy. You decide to stand next to Julie's chair and talk to her until Tommy sits down. Then you nonchalantly sit next to him. The waiter comes by with six menus.

"I want a menu," little Julie says. "It's not fair."

"Here you go," Tommy says. "Use mine. Your sister and I will share one." He looks at you and smiles. You look into his eyes and smile back. *Was that the smile of a flirt or the smile of a friend?* you wonder.

Tommy pulls his chair toward yours and leans close. Your heart is pounding so fast and so loud that you are sure he can hear it. You choose your dishes and Tommy moves his chair away. *Definitely the move of a friend,* you decide.

When dinner arrives, you notice that Tommy is using a fork. Everyone in your family uses chopsticks, even Julie.

Unaccustomed as you are to flirting, there's something about the "old friend" atmosphere that gives you the courage to say, "Hey, Tommy, didn't

(continued on page 76)

they teach you how to use chopsticks in Michigan? Let me give you a lesson."

Then, matter-of-factly, you show him how to hold his fingers and how to grip the wooden sticks.

"Thanks," he says, softly. "It's fun to eat this way."

Somewhere in the middle of the meal, Julie yells, "Let's go see *Star Wars* after dinner."

"Maybe another time, honey," your mom says. "It'll be too late by the time we finish dinner."

"I've never seen it," Tommy says. "Have you?" he asks, looking in your direction.

You have seen it three times, but you think that if you say you haven't seen it, he might ask you to go with him after dinner.

If you say you have never seen the movie, turn to page 86.

If you say that you've already seen it, turn to page 91.

You feel guilty leaving your parents with a house full of four-year-olds, so you set up another time to meet Mrs. Conroy. Then you begin to concentrate on the party. Food first.

In your house, the birthday person gets to choose the menu. In addition to peanut-butter-and-jelly sandwiches, Julie has ordered marshmallows, potato chips, M&M's, and pickles. You decide to add carrot sticks, too, as a feeble gesture to a balanced meal.

You and your mom set up a table outside. Your dad carts out the food and sets up a second table for the presents.

"Thank goodness Julie was born while it's still warm enough to have an outdoor party," says your dad.

You look up at the sky. There are dark clouds on the horizon. "Warm enough, yes. But I'm not too sure that it'll be dry enough," you say, hoping you are wrong.

"It'll be chaos if we have to bring them all into the house," says your mom. "I allowed Julie to invite fifteen kids because I knew we were going to have the party outside."

"And I planned all running and jumping games and races," you say. "We're in big trouble if we have to go inside." Twenty minutes later, just as the last child is arriving, the skies open up and torrents of rain pour down.

The kids have been running around at a feverish pitch. They race into the house screaming about the

(continued on page 78)

rain. You can just imagine what the place is going to look like when this party is over.

You, your mom, and your dad start to bring the stuff in from the yard. You suspect that you are making a terrible mistake leaving the kids on their own, but unless you get the stuff in fast, everything will be ruined. You gather up the food and cart the presents into the kitchen.

When you have finally delivered the last load, you steel yourself for disaster and walk into the living room. There, sitting on the floor flanked by fifteen four-year-olds and one giant stuffed giraffe, is Ricky. He is wearing a perfectly pressed khaki safari suit, and a big hat like the ones African hunters wear. The kids are sitting around him, wide-eyed, listening to his safari story about lions and elephants and giraffes.

When he finishes his story he looks up at you and smiles.

"What are you doing here?" you ask. "And where did the giraffe come from?"

"Didn't Julie tell you?" he asks. "She invited me to her birthday party. And she told me that she loved giraffes."

Maybe Julie isn't so bad after all, you think.

All afternoon Ricky plays with the kids—organizing games, singing songs, doing the hokey pokey. At various times, you, your mother, and your father all join in the games. Ricky is absolutely terrific with the kids and you love watching him.

(continued on page 79)

You have always been attracted to guys who like kids.

When the party guests leave, Julie won't let Ricky alone. She drags him off to look at her presents, climbs on his lap, and begs him to tell her more animal stories.

You and your father are in the kitchen cleaning up when you hear Julie say, "Now you have to take me for a ride in your car."

"Young lady," says Ricky, "*now* what I have to do is take your *sister* for a ride in my car. The birthday party is officially over."

Ricky arrives in the kitchen with Julie on his shoulders. His shirt is stained with grape juice and his pants look as though he has trekked through the jungle in them. *But he still looks great,* you think.

"How about Alan's for a lobster dinner?" he asks you.

Alan's is a beautiful restaurant that overlooks Long Island Sound. There are candles on the tables, soft music in the background, and while you eat, you can hear the waves splashing onto the sand. You were there once with your grandparents.

"Give me ten minutes to dress," you say as you race up the stairs, two at a time.

As you are driving to the restaurant, Ricky can't stop talking about how much fun he had at the party.

"I'm an only child," he says as he pulls into the parking lot. "And for most of my childhood, my

(continued on page 80)

parents were on business trips. They always came home with presents for me, but they didn't have much time for love." He stops the car and turns to you. "Your family is full of love. I'm jealous."

"Hey, don't be jealous," you say. "We always have room for one more. We could sort of adopt you."

"Well," says Ricky, taking your hands into his. "Adoption wasn't quite what I had in mind."

You look into his eyes. You feel a terrible urge to throw your arms around his neck and kiss him passionately. Instead, you smile and say, "Actually, it wasn't what I had in mind either."

Then, as if you are in a slow-motion movie, your bodies move closer and closer together until you are locked in each other's arms.

The End

"Sure," you say as you walk toward the prettiest and most popular group of girls in the school.

After introductions, Suzie says, "Hey, we're on our way to Ray's Pizza for lunch. Why don't you join us?"

You promised to have the car back by noon, and it is now eleven-forty-five. "Sorry, but I've gotta get home," you say.

"I'd better go too," says Tommy. "I don't have any wheels."

"I'll drive you home after lunch," says one of the girls.

"Great!" says Tommy. "Then I'd love to come."

"Well," you say awkwardly, "I'd better be going."

"Thanks," says Tommy. He kisses you on the forehead.

As you drive out of the parking lot, you look down the street. Tommy and the cheerleading squad are walking animatedly toward Ray's. You could kick yourself.

The End

Mark arrives at your house at a quarter past seven Saturday night. He is with a man you have never seen before.

"This is Paul," Mark says, "my cousin from Paris."

"Bonsoir, mademoiselle," he says, taking your hand and kissing it. "I am honored to meet you. I have seen many pictures of you in Mark's room. In fact," Paul says, "you photograph exquisitely."

"Thank you," you say, looking at Mark in confusion. *This was supposed to be a special night for Mark and me,* you think.

Mark just stands there smiling.

"I am here in America for my magazine," Paul says. "I am a fashion photographer for the French edition of *Vogue* magazine. I would like to shoot some pictures of you for my winter assignment. Mark told me that you would be interested, yes?"

"Interested?" you say. "That's an understatement!" You practically suffocate Mark with a hug. You wish Paul weren't there so you could kiss Mark! You are not really sure what love is, but you have a feeling that you are in love with Mark.

Aha, you suddenly think, *Paul is a Frenchman.* You put your arms around Mark and kiss him—a long, lingering kiss. When it is over, you look at Paul and smile.

"L'amour," he says. *"Toujours l'amour."*

The End

"Hello," you say, popping your head through the beaded curtain.

"Come in," Anitra's voice answers. "Welcome."

You walk into a dimly lit tent. Scarves are draped along the walls and ceiling to create a cozy, intimate atmosphere. Sparkling bits of beads and mirrors are suspended from the ceiling encircling a small table in the center of the tent.

Anitra is wearing a turban on her head. Her fingers are covered with rings; her arms with bracelets. *It's exactly what I expected,* you think, a little bit nervous.

Anitra leads you through the curtain of beads that encloses the table. In the center of the table is a crystal ball.

"I'm so glad you came," Anitra says in a soft, almost inaudible voice. "Have a seat."

You sit at the table facing her. There is a strange feeling in your stomach. You have never done this before and you are very uncomfortable. Suppose she tells you something terrible?

Anitra begins immediately. She places her hands on the crystal ball and stares alternately into your eyes and into the ball.

"There's been a big change in your life over the last few months," she says.

How does she know I lost weight? you think.

"And," she continues, "you've recently made a big decision that you are very uncomfortable with. Don't worry, it was the only thing to do."

(continued on page 84)

She's talking about Mark, you think. *This is getting spooky. It's as though she can see right into my mind.*

"Something is not good in the air," she says. "Beware of things that are red, and be cautious about your judgments."

Red? you think. But nothing comes to mind.

Before you leave, you ask Anitra how she knows these things.

"I just know," she says. "I get a feeling."

For some reason, you really believe that she does know. You've only known her for a few hours but you feel as though you could trust her with your life. She has such a calm, mysterious air about her. You thank her for the fortune and return to work.

"So tell me," Ron says, dancing around you, moving his hands. "What lies in the future? Are you going to meet a handsome prince and ride off into the sunset?" He starts laughing and keeps dancing around.

"I'm going to murder a redheaded pest," you say. *Red,* you recall. *No, she couldn't have meant him.*

You pick up your money box and walk over to the side of the booth. To avoid talking to Ron, you count your money. You are short five dollars. When you left, you had $32.50. Now, there is $27.50 in the box. You count three more times with the same results.

Ron is the only one who had access to your box. *Red,* you think again. You wonder if this is the red that Anitra warned you about.

(continued on page 85)

You are tempted to ask Ron if he took the money. You could make it sound as though you think he borrowed it or something. But he'd probably think you were accusing him of stealing—and what if he didn't have anything to do with it? Suppose you made a mistake in counting? But you are almost positive that you counted right.

Then again, Anitra warned you to be cautious about your judgments.

If you ask Ron about the money, turn to page 95.

If you wait a while before making any accusations, turn to page 101.

You gulp and then say, as quietly as possible, "I've never seen it either."

"What do you mean you haven't seen it? You did too see it. In New Hampshire with me. Remember?" says Julie.

You have a strong urge to dump the beef with black bean sauce on her bratty little head. Instead, you stammer a dumb answer.

"Oh, I didn't mean I *never* saw it," you say. "What I meant was that I could never see enough of it." *Shoot,* you think. *I really messed that one up.*

"That's good enough for me," says Tommy. "Let's go see it after dinner?"

"Great," you say, wondering if you are going to be his date or his pal.

After dinner, Tommy's folks leave you their car and everyone takes off in your car. You and Tommy walk to the movie and get in line for tickets. You wonder if he is going to pay for your ticket. You borrowed five dollars from your mother, just in case.

When you get to the front of the line, Tommy turns to you. "Uh-oh. I didn't expect to be going to a movie. I only have six dollars."

"No problem," you say. "I borrowed five from my mom."

Even though you are both stuffed, Tommy buys a container of popcorn. "Can't watch a movie without it," he says.

Together you walk into the dark theater and take your seats. As you are reaching for a handful of

(continued on page 87)

popcorn, you feel Tommy's hand on yours. Then, during the opening scene, Tommy slips his arm around your shoulders. He pulls you close to him and whispers in your ear.

"I'm glad you lied," he says. "I've been hoping we could be more than just family friends. The minute you said you had never seen *Star Wars*, I knew you'd been thinking the same thing."

You are glad the theater is dark because you know your face is bright red.

"Everyone has seen *Star Wars*," he adds. "This is my third time."

The End

"Julie, you're such a pain sometimes," you yell as you get up. *It's only Mrs. Tridel,* you think. *She will just have to suffer my beautiful face.* You walk downstairs and open the door.

"Hi," says Ricky. "You left this in my car." He is holding your camera case.

You cover your face. "I'm so embarrassed," you say. "I look like a complete disaster." *Wonderful,* you think, *my plan works and now look at me.* "Come in," you say, "I'll be right back." You run upstairs to wash your face and put on some decent clothes.

"Who's at the door?" Julie says running past you.

"I thought you were watching TV," you say.

When you return downstairs, you find Ricky surrounded by wooden blocks.

"We're building a tower," Julie informs you. "He's a better builder than you are," she says.

"Julie," you say, "go watch TV."

"I don't want to."

"If you put all of these blocks down in a row, you can make an airport ramp," Ricky says, setting up some blocks.

"Would you like something to drink?" you ask, feeling like an intruder.

"I'll have some chocolate milk," Julie says.

"Not *you,*" you say, ready to strangle her.

"That sounds good," Ricky says. "Make that two." You go into the kitchen to get the drinks. *Stupid sister,* you think. *Four-year-olds aren't good for anything.*

(continued on page 89)

When you return, Ricky and Julie are building a railroad. *That's the last time I let that little brat stay up,* you think. You didn't leave your camera case in his car so that he could come and play blocks with Julie.

"Time for you to go to sleep," you say.

"No, it's my birthday tomorrow. Can't I just stay up a little longer?" Julie whines.

"No," you say. "Now."

"Well, I better be going anyway," Ricky says. "I've got a bunch of things to do."

You say goodbye to Ricky and thank him again. When he leaves, you are ready to drag your sister upstairs by the hair.

"I like your friend," she says. "He's fun."

"I'm so glad you think so," you say, biting your lip. "But it looked as though he was your friend."

The next day you are still furious at Julie and upset with everything that happened. You will never see Ricky again now. You never even got to have a conversation with him! You get up early and storm out of the house without even wishing Julie a happy birthday.

After taking care of some errands, you drive to the Conroys' house to drop off the party pictures. No one is home. You drop the envelope through the mail slot and drive home. Julie's birthday party is set for three o'clock and you've agreed to help out. But right now, doing anything nice for Julie does not appeal to you.

At noontime, Mrs. Conroy calls to tell you that

(continued on page 90)

she loves the pictures you dropped off that morning.

"I'm going to the office today. Why don't you come pick out some clothes while I'm there?" she says. "Those pictures are so fantastic that I've decided to throw in some bonus stuff."

If you go shopping, turn to page 98.

If you help out at the party, turn to page 77.

"I loved it," you say. "I've seen it three times."

"I loved it, too," says your mother. And the conversation moves on.

"Excuse me," Tommy says, standing up. "I'll be right back." He walks toward the rest room. A few minutes later he returns, smiling.

When dinner is finished, you can barely move. *I'm going to have to starve for the next week,* you think. *Thank goodness there's no dessert.*

Suddenly the lights dim and eight waiters march out of the kitchen. One of them is carrying a bowl of ice cream with a candle stuck in the middle.

"Happy birthday to you. Happy birthday . . ."

You are wondering whose birthday it is when the waiters place the ice cream in front of you. You look around, confused. Then you look at Tommy. There's that same mischievous smile he used to wear when he threw spiders at you.

You smile and thank the waiters. When they leave, Tommy laughs. It's the same old laugh; only now you like it.

During the next week, Tommy drives you up the wall. You can't figure out where you stand with him. On Thursday he calls you up and asks you to come with him to get his hair cut. *Very romantic,* you think.

"I might do something drastic if you don't come," he says. Naturally, you go. Afterward, the two of you go to lunch and he takes the check.

At seven-thirty the next morning, he calls. "I'll be

(continued on page 92)

over in five minutes," he says. "We're going jogging." You get up and throw on a pair of sweats. When he arrives, he gets out of the car with a fishing pole.

"I decided that fishing is more fun," he says. *He's nuts,* you think. *But I guess that's why I like him.*

While you and Tommy fish, you giggle, laugh, and sing. The fish don't come anywhere near you. Neither does Tommy.

After fishing, Tommy asks you to help him find a birthday present for his mom. You change out of your sweats and Tommy drives to the mall.

"I'll be right back," Tommy says and runs into a pet store. You sit down on a bench and wait.

You are brushing your hair when a small man walks up to you. "Hello," he says. "My name is Stephen Mansell. Have you ever done any modeling?"

"No," you answer.

"You haven't?" he says. "That surprises me. A beautiful girl like you." You feel yourself blush. "Well," he continues, "I'm with the M&T Advertising Agency." He hands you a business card. "You're absolutely perfect for the jeans ad that I'm working on. I would love you to come down to my studio so I could see how you photograph."

"Really?" you say, amazed at the offer.

"Of course. Why don't you come down tomorrow morning at ten? I'll have my makeup artist do your face and my designer fit you for clothes."

"Okay," you say.

(continued on page 93)

"Great," he says. "The address is on the card. I'll see you tomorrow."

You watch as he walks away. *It's great being skinny,* you think, and you race toward the pet shop to tell Tommy.

Just as you get there, he is walking out, carrying a parrot in a cage. "Look," he says. "It was on sale. My mom will love it, don't you think?"

"I hope so," you say. "Guess what happened?" You tell him about the guy and show him the card.

"You're not going," he says.

"What do you mean I'm not going."

"You don't know who this guy is," he says. "You can't go."

"Don't tell me what I can do," you say. "I shouldn't even have told you." You walk away, with Tommy following.

"Listen, I don't want anything to happen to you." His voice is gentle. "Tell you what. I'll take you sailing tomorrow instead. What do you say?"

You look at his face. The mischief is gone. There is a serious, intense look in his eyes.

If you choose to go sailing, turn to page 111.

If you decide to go to the modeling studio, turn to page 106.

"Julie," you yell. "I don't care what you're doing. I can't go to the door like this. Go answer it and get the package. And don't forget to say thank you."

You hear a grumble and then Julie bounds down the stairs. "The polka-dotted monster," she sings.

Five minutes later Julie runs into your room and hands you a camera case. Your eyes light up.

"Who gave this to you?" you ask anxiously.

"I don't know, some tall guy. He says that you left it in his car."

"Well, is he still down there?" you ask.

"No, I told him that you weren't home. You said you didn't want anyone to see you!"

Well, you think, *that's the end of that. The scheme worked and I blew it.*

The End

"Ron," you say, "were you here the whole time I was gone?"

"Yeah, of course I was."

"Well, before I left I counted my money and now there's five dollars missing."

"Are you accusing me or something? You probably counted wrong. After all, you aren't perfect," he says.

Maybe I did jump to conclusions, you think. *It is possible that I miscounted.* You decide that you are not going to pursue it further. You've done what you can.

"Yeah, you're probably right," you say, "Forget it."

"It's hot in here," Ron says to you a few minutes later.

"Do you want a soda?" you say, trying to forget the money. "I'll get us two drinks."

You leave the booth before Ron answers and run over to the hot dog stand.

After waiting in line for a few minutes, you pick up the drinks and return to your booth.

"Thanks," Ron says, "but don't think that makes up for what you said. I'm taking a break. See you later."

Why did I get stuck with such a creep? you think.

You pick up your money box and walk toward the back. You decide to check one last time and— wait a minute—now you come up with the whole $32.50.

(continued on page 96)

Ron must have put it back, you think. *Anitra was right about red.*

"Which stuffed animal would you like me to win, honey?" says a customer to his date.

You look up to see Chris, the creepy schoolmate you met in the parking lot.

"Oh, look who's working here," he says. "It's Fatty in a new body. Get ready to give me a prize."

How about a baseball in your face? you say to yourself.

He is standing with a tall, beautiful girl who tosses her long blond hair and says, "Oh, Chris, win me the elephant."

You have seen this girl at school and have never heard an intelligent word out of her mouth. *She must have brains,* you think, *but they're probably in her feet.* You wonder how anyone could spend more than five minutes with a jerk like Chris.

"One set of balls will do," Chris says. "I'm a pro at this game."

"I can't wait to get the elephant," chirps the girl.

"Don't worry about a thing, baby," says Chris. "Just give me the balls."

Chris is probably the single most obnoxious person you have ever known. As you are reaching for the baseballs, a brilliant idea pops into your head. If you put your foot on the pedal, the rabbits won't move. The pedal is generally used to bring all the rabbits back in place after someone knocks them down, but it *could* be used to prevent a player's knocking down any rabbits at all.

(continued on page 97)

You know that fixing the game so Chris can't win would be dishonest. On the other hand, Chris is such a monstrous creature that he doesn't deserve to win at anything. You think about all the nasty things he has said to you over the years. It would kill you to have to give that creep a prize.

If you fix the game, turn to page 112.

If you let him play fairly, turn to page 118.

You are thrilled to have a legitimate excuse to miss Julie's party. At twelve-thirty you hop into the car and drive to the Conroy showroom. Mrs. Conroy greets you.

"Can I try things on?" you ask.

"Of course," says Mrs. Conroy. "I'll be your fashion consultant."

You are thrilled. Until now you have always worn heavy sweaters and blouses that don't tuck in. People have always told you that vertical stripes are more flattering than horizontal stripes, that dark colors are better on people who have "figure problems." Finally you don't have to worry about "flattering lines." You are thin, and no matter what you wear, you are not going to look fat.

Mrs. Conroy is terrific. She helps you put together outfits, tells you how to use scarves and accessories, and she doesn't stop telling you how stunning you look.

When you walk out of Conroy's you have three boxes of clothes—a whole wardrobe for your new self. Mrs. Conroy kept insisting that you take more. If you had had to buy all that stuff in a store, it would have cost at least $200. Thanks to your photography skills, you paid nothing.

You are deliriously happy when you burst through the door of your house. The party is over and Julie and one of her friends are sitting in the living room surrounded by presents. There is a giant stuffed giraffe standing between the girls.

(continued on page 99)

"What an incredible animal," you say, petting the giraffe, which is taller than you are. "Who gave it to you?"

"My friend Richard," says Julie.

"Richard?" you say. "You don't have any friend named Richard."

"I do too," says Julie. "And he came to my party and played games with us all afternoon." Then when everybody left he took me and Jennie for a ride in his orange car."

"Car?" you say. "Oh, no. Do you mean Ricky? Is that who it was? Ricky? The guy who was here the other day to see *me*."

"That's the one," says Julie. "Except I call him Richard, and he was here because I invited him to my birthday party."

You can feel yourself bursting. You do not know whom you are angrier at—yourself or your little sister. You throw your boxes on the couch and collapse on the floor. *All dressed up and nowhere to go,* you think.

The End

You look at this thing standing next to you. "I can't go to lunch," you say. "I have to get back to work."

"You are unfortunate, my dear. I will haunt you forever," he says, dancing around you.

"Who are you?" you ask.

"That you will never know!" he says. And he runs back into the Haunted House.

The End

You hesitate to make an accusation without some proof. If you are wrong, you know you will feel horrible. You decide to let it slide and you hide your box in a corner and stand up front.

"It's my turn to break," says Ron and he takes off.

As you stand there, you look across at the roller coaster. The sandy-haired guy is still there. In fact, he is looking directly at you and smiling. You smile back and then look away. You don't want him to think you are staring at him.

While you mindlessly run the booth, you keep thinking about what Anitra said about red. You wonder if she can tell you more. When Ron returns from his break, you go back into Anitra's tent.

"Well, hello," she says.

"Anitra," you say, "when you told me to beware of red, did you have something or someone on your mind?"

"Well, yes. But I didn't want to be specific."

"Would it by any chance be Ron, the guy I work with?" you say.

"It is," she says. "He's not an honest person."

"How do you know?" you say.

"I just do. He gives out bad vibes. I don't know what you have to beware of, but be careful."

You are dying to ask more questions, but your dialogue is interrupted when a boy limps into the tent, crying.

"What happened, Damian?" Anitra says, picking him up. There is blood dripping from his foot. His

(continued on page 102)

crying crescendos. "I better take him to get this fixed," she says to you. "May I ask you a favor?"

"Sure," you say.

"Would you watch my tent for a moment while I bring my son to the first-aid room? You can put on some clothes from that box and tell people I'll be right back."

"Sure," you say, intrigued with the idea of dressing up like a fortune-teller. You put on a long sequined dress that jangles when you move, a navy-blue turban, and a thick black veil. Then you pile on the jewelry. You feel as though you are playing dress-up in your grandmother's attic.

Just as you sit down in Anitra's seat, a hand separates the beaded curtain at the entrance.

"Hello," a male voice says. And in walks the roller coaster guy, the one who looks like a young Paul Newman. Luckily you are wearing a veil.

"Can you tell me my fortune?" he asks.

If you tell his fortune, turn to page 104.

If you tell him to come back later, turn to page 109.

"Will you take off your mask before we go to lunch?" you ask.

"Are you going to go?" he says.

"Okay, I'll go," you say, your curiosity getting the better of you.

"Now that's the type of girl I like," he says. "One with nerves! Here goes nothing," says the werewolf and he lifts off his mask.

You are in shock. Words won't come out of your mouth. The only thing you can do is stare and smile. This horribly ugly beast has turned out to be the gorgeous blond guy that you have been flirting with all day.

It's kind of like a fairy tale, you think, as he takes your hand and you walk together toward the pizza house. *But instead of a frog, it's a werewolf who has turned into a prince.*

The End

"Have a seat," you say, and he sits down across from you. Your stomach has butterflies; your hand is jittery. You cannot quite believe you are doing this. Thank goodness that veil is covering your face.

You look into the crystal ball and then into his eyes. They are a clear, soft blue. The dim red light gives his face a pinkish glow, and his blue shirt matches his eyes.

"There are many ups and downs in your life," you begin, picturing the roller coaster. "But you will always land on your feet."

He smiles.

"Your distant future is going to be very success-ful. You are going to earn much money and have great happiness."

"What about my near future?" he asks.

"Hmm," you say. "The crystal ball tells me that you are going to meet someone today." You hesi-tate. "This person will be very important to you in the future, so pay special attention. You will meet this person at approximately five o'clock. You must watch carefully."

"Wow," he says. "I better keep my eyes open. This was fun. I enjoyed it. Thanks a lot." He hands you a dollar.

"Keep it," you say. "This was my present to you."

"Thanks," he says. "If you ever want to ride the roller coaster, you can ride free."

You don't mention the incident to Anitra when she returns, but you immediately plan to take a five

(continued on page 105)

o'clock break. You have every intention of becoming this important person in his life.

At five minutes to five you begin to stroll toward the roller coaster. You notice that he is glancing around, as though he is expecting someone. Your plan seems to be working.

Just then a girl walks over to him. They talk. They laugh. And then, you watch as the two of them walk off together. *That was supposed to be me*, you think.

You should have known better. Only gypsies can tell fortunes!

The End

There is no way you are going to let this opportunity slide by. You have always wanted to model, and this may be your only chance.

"Call me in the morning and I'll let you know about sailing," you say to Tommy. Your mind is made up, but you don't feel like being lectured.

All the way home Tommy tries to convince you to go sailing. You close your ears.

The next morning you get up at eight. You blow-dry your hair and curl it. You put on a black wool skirt and a white blouse. Then you stand in front of the mirror and admire your figure. You twist your torso, tilt your head, lean seductively against the wall and imagine yourself in *Vogue* magazine.

Suddenly you remember that Tommy is going to call so you take the phone off the hook. You've made up your mind and you are not going to change it.

You skip breakfast so that you'll be very thin, and you tell your mother that you are meeting Jill. Once you are in the car, you take out the card and look at the address. It is in a part of town that you hardly ever visit, and you take a couple of wrong turns before you finally find the street. As you get closer to the address, you notice that the houses are getting shabbier. Finally you pull up to a small gray building. There is a sign on the front door that says M & T.

You can feel butterflies in your stomach as you knock on the door. You wonder if Tommy was

(continued on page 107)

right. Are you getting yourself into trouble by being here? *Oh well,* you think. *It's too late now.* Just then Stephen Mansell opens the door.

"You came!" he says, as if he is surprised.

"You told me to," you say.

He motions you to a room filled with camera equipment and various shaded backgrounds. The lights that are set up are the same as the ones you work with in your photography class. There is a screen with red fabric panels in the far corner and two closed doors in the back. In the front of the screen is an overstuffed yellow chair and a table.

"Where are the other people?" you ask.

"Other people?" he says.

"Yes. The makeup person and the designer."

"Oh, they'll be coming in soon. I'll get you started," he says. You have a creepy feeling about the place. It's a lot smaller than you expected.

"I'll be right back with some clothes for you to try on." The man walks into one of the closed rooms and shuts the door.

There is a portfolio lying on the table. You open it. The first page is a picture of a girl wearing jeans and a sweatshirt. She is beautiful and the photography is well done. The next few pictures are of the same girl in different bathing suits. After that, there is a different girl and more bathing suits. Altogether there are five models, all wearing skimpy bikinis. They are pictured in very seductive poses.

You suddenly become frightened. You really

(continued on page 108)

don't want to pose in a bathing suit in front of this man. You close the book and look around.

Where is the makeup artist? The clothing designer? you wonder. *There is no one here except this little man who came up to me in a shopping mall.*

If you leave immediately, before Stephen Mansell comes back, turn to page 117.

If you do not want to insult him by just walking out, turn to page 114.

"Listen," you say. "The woman who tells fortunes will be back in about ten minutes. Why don't you come back then?"

"Oh, really," this blue-eyed guy says as he tilts his head. "Can't you tell my fortune?"

Your heart is beating fast. "No," you say. "I'm just watching the shop."

"Okay," he says. "That's too bad. I'll try and come back later." He walks out.

I blew it, you think. *That was my big chance!* You throw your turban back in the box.

When Anitra returns, you tell her what happened. She laughs.

"It will work for the best," she says. "Thank you for everything. And again, I warn you of red. Take a firm stand on your feelings."

You return to work and pick up your money box. Now you count only $22.50. Another five dollars is missing! *That's it,* you think. Ron has been in the booth both times you were gone. And each time five dollars has disappeared. You don't want to say anything directly to him because you are sure he would only deny it; but you know that you have to do something.

"Take a firm stand on your feelings," you remember.

At four o'clock, your boss comes around to check on everything. You take him aside and tell him what has been happening. He promises to take care of it.

(continued on page 110)

The next day when you arrive at the booth you see the back of a male. This male has sandy hair. When you get closer, he turns around. Your mouth drops open.

"Hi," the roller coaster guy says. "I just got word that I had to switch jobs with some guy who used to work here. My name is Bob."

You pinch yourself to see if you are dreaming.

"It's funny," Bob continues. "I had my fortune told yesterday, and the woman said that I would find baseball and romance in my future. And here I am in a baseball booth already."

You smile at Anitra's prediction. *I'll handle the second part,* you think. *No problem at all.*

The End

You wake up the next morning to rain pounding on your windows. *So much for sailing,* you think. *What now?* At nine-thirty the phone rings.

"I hope you're hungry!" Tommy says. "I'll be over in ten minutes."

You put on a pair of jeans and go into the kitchen. There is a note taped to the refrigerator. *We're at the Kaufmans' helping them settle in. Mom, Dad, and Julie.*

Hmm, you think. *He knows I'm alone.*

Tommy arrives a few minutes later with two grocery bags full of food. "You go make a fire," he says. "Leave the cooking to me."

"Yes, sir," you say.

Thirty-five minutes later, Tommy sets two glasses of orange juice in front of the blazing fire. Next he brings two plates, exquisitely arranged with eggs Benedict, hash browns, sausages, and two sprigs of parsley.

"How come such royal treatment?" you ask.

"Because you're you!" he says and he kisses you lightly on the lips. "When that man asked you to model yesterday, I suddenly realized how important you were to me."

The fire crackles in the background as you hold hands and eat your breakfasts.

And to think it all began with a dead cat!

The End

"Well, are you going to get me the balls or do I have to get them myself?" Chris says to you.

That's it, you think to yourself.

"Here you go," you say. "Three out of three wins you a prize." You hand him the balls and put your foot on the pedal.

"No problem," he says as he takes the balls.

What an arrogant fool, you think.

He throws the first ball. It hits a rabbit and nothing happens.

Then he tosses the next two balls. The rabbits wiggle but remain upright.

"Give me another set," he commands as he hands you another fifty cents.

You pass him another set of balls.

"Come on, Chris. I just have to have that elephant," the girl says.

After two more sets of balls, Chris gives up. "This thing is a ripoff," he says. "The rabbits don't move."

"Sure they do," you say. You take your foot off the pedal and throw a ball at a rabbit. It falls over.

"Let's go," Chris says, grabbing the girl by the arm.

"Wait," you call. "You forgot your prize." You pick up a plastic spider and hand it to the girl.

"Yuck," she says. "Why would I want that?" She and Chris stomp away.

When they are out of sight, a funny thing happens to you. You had expected to be rolling on the floor

(continued on page 113)

in hysterics; but instead you feel rotten. You were so angry at Chris that you stooped to his level. Now you are angry at yourself for having been dishonest.

You can't believe how easily you compromised your values. It's true, you succeeded in humiliating Chris, but you also dragged yourself down in the process.

The End

You decide that you've been warped by too many scary movies. *An overactive imagination,* you think. Stephen Mansell is a little man who looks as though he couldn't harm a fly. He's older than your father! And he's been courteous to you right from the beginning. You'll just wait for him to come back. If things don't seem right, then you'll leave.

A few minutes later he returns. "I've got a few pairs of jeans for you to try on," he says.

You take the jeans. *Maybe he really is doing an ad,* you think.

"You can change behind the screen," he says, pointing to the corner of the room.

You walk behind the screen. There is no door to close, no lock to lock. Even though you know he can't see through the panels, you are very uncomfortable changing in such an open place. Nonetheless, you try on three pairs of jeans and come out wearing the best-fitting pair.

"Gorgeous," he says. "After you put this on," he adds, handing you a blue-and-white tube top, "we'll take some shots."

You go behind the screen and slip on the top. It is very tight, and you feel extremely self-conscious. "It's too small," you call. "Do you have another one?"

"Let me see," he says, walking behind the screen without even warning you. "Oh, that's perfect. Now come over here and lie down on this blanket." You follow his directions.

(continued on page 115)

"Just relax," he says. You are shaking all over. You don't like this, but you are afraid to walk out. He shoots a few pictures and then hands you a small box. "Go put this on." You take the box.

"You are perfect," he says as he watches you walk toward the screen. "Absolutely stunning. Your body is spectacular."

That's it, you think. You are going to put on your own clothes and leave. The man frightens you.

Out of curiosity, you open the box and take out a string bikini. *A jeans ad,* you think. *Sure. No way I'm going to put this on!*

"I have a few more things for you," he says. "I'll be right back." You hear him close the door on the other side of the room.

You quickly throw your clothes on and step out from behind the screen. He's nowhere in sight. You are shaking as you approach the door.

"Where are you going?" he says from behind you. "We aren't finished yet!"

You are speechless. You run toward the door and fling it open, fumbling for your keys as you run. Tears are streaming down your face as you near your car. You can hear footsteps behind you.

"But, darling," he says, "we've just begun." Suddenly a car screeches to a halt. Tommy jumps out and runs to you. You hold him tightly, tears rolling down your cheeks. Stephen turns and scurries back into his building without another word.

"Don't try to talk," says Tommy, hugging you.

(continued on page 116)

You cannot believe how good it feels to be in his strong arms. "Get in my car," he says, opening the door. "I'll come back for yours later."

When you are both inside, he turns to you. "I was so worried!" he says, taking you in his arms again. "I can't lose the only girl who would put up with my craziness. What would I do without you?"

And then he lifts your chin and presses his lips to yours. You hold him with all your strength. His lips are soft and gentle; his body is strong and powerful. You have never felt so safe and so loved.

The End

There are no ad layouts in the book and no sign of published work anywhere—just photographs of girls your age in all sorts of seductive poses. *How stupid can I be?* you think. *I'm certainly not going to hang around to see what this man has in mind for me.*

You grab your purse and walk toward the door. Your hand is shaking as you turn the knob. When you get outside, your walk turns into a run.

You are just getting into your car when Stephen Mansell walks out of the building. Shaking, you turn the key in the ignition. The car doesn't start.

"Where are you going?" he yells.

Please start, you think, as you try again.

"Don't you want me to take some pictures?" he calls as you pull away. You don't even look back.

You are still shaking when you arrive home. Terrifying images flash through your mind—YOUNG GIRL FOUND MURDERED—LOCAL TEEN-AGER MISSING. *He never even asked my name,* you think. *How dumb could I be?*

You lie down on your bed and burst into tears.

The End

This is my job, you think. *I won't stoop to cheating, no matter how much he deserves it.* You hand him three balls and hope he misses.

"Watch this," he says to the blonde. "That elephant's as good as yours." Then he pitches the first two balls and knocks down two rabbits in a row.

You feel sick to your stomach. *Come on. Miss, miss, miss!* you say to yourself as he aims the third ball.

Then, just as he is tossing the ball, Ron arrives at the counter with a girl in a bikini. Chris glances over, loses his concentration, and throws wild.

Yahoo! you think to yourself. "Oh, what a pity," you say out loud. "Foiled by your roving eye."

"Jerk," says the blonde as she drags him away.

That's probably the only intelligent thought she's ever had, you think. Then you glance at Ron. *And that's probably the cleverest thing you've ever done*, you think. *And you don't even know you did it!*

The End

About the Author

BOYS! BOYS! BOYS! is JAN GELMAN's second book; her first was SUMMER IN THE SUN, *A Follow Your Heart Romance #1*. Jan is nineteen and a junior at the University of Colorado, Boulder.

In writing BOYS! BOYS! BOYS!, Jan called upon her own high school experiences and those of her friends. Like the heroine, Jan once managed a football team; she is also an avid photographer.

Jan loves to travel. She has visited nearly every one of the United States: she has camped in California, skied in Vermont, vacationed on a houseboat in Colorado, and hiked in the Berkshire Mountains of Massachusetts.

"Someday," says Jan, "I hope to bike and backpack my way around the world."